THE WORLD AFTER

Book One

RYAN CASEY

Higher Bank Books

The characters and events portrayed in this book are fictitious. Any similarity to real persons, living or dead, is coincidental and not intended by the author. Any reference to real locations is only for atmospheric effect, and in no way truly represents those locations.

Copyright © 2017 by Ryan Casey

Cover design by Damonza

All rights reserved.

No part of this book may be reproduced in any form or by any electronic or mechanical means, including information storage and retrieval systems, without written permission from the author, except for the use of brief quotations in a book review.

Published by Higher Bank Books

If you want to be notified when Ryan Casey's next novel is released and receive an exclusive free book from his Dead Days post apocalyptic series, please sign up to his mailing list.

http://ryancaseybooks.com/fanclub

Your email address will never be shared and you can unsubscribe at any time.

THE WORLD AFTER

Book One

PROLOGUE

NASA HQ

Washington, DC.

SADIA BAILEY always expected the world would come to an end someday. But, like everyone else, she never really thought she'd see it in her lifetime.

The weather indicator on the bottom right of her computer monitor said it was ninety-three degrees outside the NASA headquarters in Washington, DC. A day this scorching in Washington was a rarity, something that only came along every now and then during the summer. Sure, they had good summers, but compared to the likes of Florida and further south, they were just outside the ideal sunshine territory.

But it didn't matter to Sadia or anyone else inside NASA's headquarters. There were no windows deep in the offices, in the underbelly of this place—just lots and lots of windows into the worlds of space in the form of computer screens. There were no sounds of birds chirping, or people having fun and enjoying themselves in the summer sun. Just the tapping of keyboards, the muffled mumbles of conversation.

And right now, all of those computers screens were focused on one thing in particular.

S_{4573}.

"Now, there should be a level of concern," Mr Boston, her project manager, said, standing at the front of the offices with his hands to his sides. He was wearing his white shirt, stains under his pits, sweat covering his forehead. He sure looked like he could do with getting outside and getting some fresh air right now. "As with all solar events, we have to exercise some caution."

Sadia could understand Boston's concern. After all, solar storms could be devastating things. Whether the general public realised it or not, it wasn't dictators that held the biggest threat to the planet. It wasn't any other kind of outside solar event, like an asteroid or meteor. It wasn't terrorism or nuclear bravado.

It was the sun itself.

"Back in 2012," Boston said, "a massive solar flare was kicked out of the sun, followed shortly by a coronal mass ejection —or CME."

The screens all changed to digital imagery of the solar event, which was enough to give Sadia the shivers.

"That CME gave off enough energy to cause total devastation across America and the rest of the world."

The screen changed again, this time to a map of the USA. On that map, there was a whole load of dots showing the particular systems that would be affected by the flares. Suffice to say, that map was absolutely packed. America would be devastated. The rest of the world would follow.

"If that solar storm had hit us, the devastation would've been unprecedented. We're talking about fifty times the costs of Hurricane Katrina. But money would be the least of the world's problems. The time it would take to fix the world's power grid would be unlike any other mission humanity has ever faced. The majority of society would be without power for months... in the best case scenario. Years in a realistic scenario. And in a worst case scenario... well."

He didn't continue. Sadia knew what Mr Boston was talking about. Everyone did.

The worst case scenario?

A global blackout. Forever.

"Now, CMEs have hit in the past. The largest was the Carrington Event in 1859. A solar flare and CME double-team destroyed all the hard telegraph work the world had established at that time. But that was 1859. This is the 2010s. Think of the infrastructural changes since then. And think about the devastation that could be caused to society."

Sadia Bailey thought about it, long and hard. She looked at the theatrical-looking image on her screen, now. A large, blackened sun, with huge waves of solar energy coming off it.

"The 2012 solar flare missed Earth by a whisker," Mr Boston said, walking to the front of the room now. "But who's to say the next one won't hit? Who's to say the next one won't be the one to send us right back to the dark ages?"

Mr Boston caught Sadia's eye. Just for a second, she saw the sincerity in his expression, like he was really, really worried about what he was talking about.

And then the lights flicked on, and he smiled. "But like I say. It's unlikely it'll hit. We have provisions in place to prevent it happening, even if by a chance of nature it does get close. For now, we just keep calm and carry on, okay? Sure. You have a good day, folks. Stay vigilant, but stay relaxed. I need a breath of fresh air."

Sadia let go of her breath and returned to her computer screen.

"Man," Mike said, leaning over to Sadia. "Talk about the conspiracy brigade showing up here."

"Hey," Sadia said, logging into her emails. "You know as well as I do just how dangerous a solar flare could be."

Mike held out his palms. "Well, yeah. But it's not like it's ever gonna happen, is it? I mean, we've got systems to detect this shit. That's what he always glosses over in his little melodramatic speeches. We've got stuff like STEREO A and B to research these things. And we've got ways to prepare people, even if this kinda thing did go down."

He crunched down on an apple and leaned his feet against his desk.

All Sadia could do was nod.

She looked at the screen, at the image of that July 2012 solar flare, and remembered what Boston had said about the Carrington Event in 1859.

The sheer devastation that had caused. And that was in a time before Edison created the lightbulb. Those were the days where the media could use paper to control people, and where everyone didn't rely on digital money and digital identities and digital *everything*.

"Just relax," Mike said, closing the solar flare imagery and opening up a video game in the far right edge of his screen. "This flare's gonna miss. All our systems have it narrowly missing."

"And that gives us a right not to warn people?"

"Warning people just scares people. We'd be causing unnecessary hysteria."

Sadia nodded. She was still unconvinced. Something was still getting to her.

"And if it *does* hit?"

Mike turned to her then. He leaned in close.

"Then the end times have arrived!" he said, in a sarcastic, forced voice.

He started laughing, and Sadia couldn't help grinning, too.

Mike was right. She was just being paranoid. They had the best systems in the world right here, for this sort of thing. There was no way that solar flare was going to affect Earth. Maybe one day, just not anytime soon.

She kept on telling herself that when she left work later that night, and as she walked down the corridor, the lights flickered.

CHAPTER ONE

Manchester, U.K.

I TOOK a deep breath and waited for the interview that I knew would make or break my life.

Let's be honest. Judging by my recent luck, it was probably going to be a life breaker rather than a life-maker.

I sat in a hallway that I'd walked through so many times. I'd always walked past these brown chairs and observed just how uncomfortable they looked. Kind of like those chairs you're made to sit on when you're in the lower years of school. The sort that creak when you sit on them, the plastic seeming ready to snap at any moment.

It was a rare stifling hot day in Manchester. Outside, I could hear the collective impatience of people stuck in their cars, honking their horns at one another so they could get home and to the beer fridges quicker. Inside here, though—my workplace at Holmes & Wisdom Media, a private company that had recently just been taken over as part of a merger—it was stifling.

The smell of sweat was strong in the air. Some of it mine, I had to concede. But not all of it, at least I hoped. Some of it had to belong to the three other people sitting by my side, they too waiting to be interviewed.

The silence in this corridor stretched on. Nobody had said a word to one another. I couldn't blame them, to be honest. What were they supposed to say? *"Hey, Scott. I'm Danny. I'm the guy who's trying to get the job you've had for the last eight years. Nice to meet you. I'll stab you in the back when you turn around, okay?"*

No. Nobody said anything. Of course they didn't. There were just the occasional moments of awkward eye contact followed by the inevitable fake smile and nods. The tapping of feet. The scratching of backs of necks. The glances at watches.

I didn't know why I was so afraid, to be honest. My old boss, Gavin, had given me an absolutely resounding reference. I worked in SEO and content management, and as far as SEO and content management went, I was pretty damn good at it. Not very good at anything that *didn't* involve SEO and content management, whether that be keeping in touch with his friends, socialising with women, or pretty much any work that could credibly be reclassified as exercise.

But everybody had their strengths, and everybody had their weaknesses.

I just happened to be so weak in every other area.

Including interviews...

"Scott Harvard?"

I lifted my head and jolted to my feet right away. "Yes? Yes?"

The woman at the door—I recognised her as Sally, one of the new people from West Brook Media, the new owners—smiled sympathetically at me, tortoiseshell glasses dangling around her neck on a little beaded chain. "We're ready for you," she said.

I rubbed the back of my head. My face felt like it was on fire. My heart raced at a million miles an hour. I had this. I just had to be myself. I knew my stuff. I had nothing at all to worry about.

I glanced back at the three people waiting in line. All looked more chilled than me. All looking better dressed, younger (even if I *was* only thirty-one), and more qualified (as true or false as that may be) than me.

I smiled at them.

All three of them shot fake smiles back at me.

Then, I followed Sally into the room that I knew would define the rest of my life.

Well. Maybe not so dramatic. But it was a pretty big deal that I got this job here. After all, I didn't fancy my chances of getting a job elsewhere. Not with the way my nerves were these days.

When I walked into the room, I noticed the immediate drop in light, and I realised it was because the blinds had been closed. The interview room resembled an interrogation room more than it did the casual, airy meeting area that I'd sat at so many times before.

At the opposite side of the desk, I saw two people. One was Gregg Warburts, the new owner. The other was...

My stomach dropped.

"Where's..." I started, then stopped right away because I realised even questioning where Gavin was revealed an element of weakness.

But I was already too late.

"Gavin is sick," the woman said. "Came down with a sudden bout of stomach cramps. So I'm sitting in for him today. Is that okay with you?"

I saw the fake smile on Julia Wilkinson's face and I knew I was screwed, right then.

"Sure," I said, pulling back a chair—which scraped across the floor. "Let's get this done with."

"In a hurry to be somewhere else, Scott?"

"No, I just... Just a figure of speech."

Julia waved a hand at me. "It's okay. I'm just teasing you." She looked down at the folder in front of her. "Anyway. I suppose we should begin."

She started with a few stock questions just to ease me in. The usual, like my prior experience (none), my passion for the job (above average, I thought). All of it was pretty straightforward. But the problem was, Julia Wilkinson hated me because I'd stood against her when she'd been trying to climb the ladder at Holmes & Wisdom. She took my move, although nothing more than a career step, as an attack of loyalty, and had been trying to turn the knife ever since even though she'd ended up on top. If it wasn't for Gavin, I wasn't sure I'd even still be here at all.

"Anyway, we'd like just to provide you with a hypothetical coding issue. If you could take a look at the code on the left and the website on the right, and establish where in the code the problem is, then that would be fantastic."

I froze. "But I..."

Julia narrowed her eyes. "Are you trying to say something, Scott?"

My heart thumped and my collar suddenly felt very tight around my neck. I loosened it, shook my head and smiled, then pulled the laptop close so I could get a better look. "Of course not," I said. "I'll... I'll take a look."

She smiled at me again. Of course she did. She knew damn well I didn't know how to code. I'd be frigging surprised if *anyone* here at Holmes & Wisdom knew how to code. Coding wasn't what we did. We purchased themes and customised them visually. We didn't mess around with HTML or CSS unless it was very basic stuff.

But still, I could see Gregg Warburts watching me, silently, his big bald head and his massive hands intimidating in their sheer size.

If I wanted to win him over, here was my chance.

I squinted at the website on the right. I couldn't see any

immediate problems, so I looked back to the left. Then I looked right again, and left again, and then right again.

I glanced up over the screen, sweat building on my forehead.

"Everything okay?" Julia asked.

"Yeah," I lied, loosening my collar once again, "just... just double-checking I've, um..."

I realised after a solid minute—which felt like an hour—that I was stuffed. There was no way I was winning this battle. So I had to take plan B. Honesty followed by passion.

"Look," I said, sliding the laptop back towards Julia. "I have to be honest. I didn't see the problem. But that's because CSS and HTML and all that coding stuff haven't really been at the forefront of Holmes & Wisdom operations over the last eight years. However, there were a lot of things I didn't know when I started working here, and which I've learned and am now exceptionally adept at. I'm sure, if West Brook Media want to take our business in a more coding hands-on direction, then I would be able to adapt to that shift in no time."

I saw the blank stares from the three of them. I saw the surprise on Gregg's face.

But mostly, I saw the slight look of victory on Julia's face. Like she'd won this battle.

"Okay," she said, closing her notepad. Gregg and Sally soon followed, then they stood. "Well, we'd like to thank you for your time, Scott."

"Wait," I said. "The coding problem. Just out of curiosity. What was it?"

Julia glanced at Gregg, who raised his eyebrows. Sally cleared her throat and looked away.

Then Julia looked right at me. "The coding problem wasn't a coding problem at all. If you'd looked closely, you'd have seen that the copy was riddled with spelling errors and that the company logo was upside-down."

My stomach turned, and I felt like a hole was opening up beneath me. "Wait. I... I saw that."

"You had an opportunity to say you'd seen it. You didn't."

"I—You said coding."

"A logo upside down? That *is* technically coding."

"But—but I—"

"Goodbye, Mr Harvard," Gregg said.

It was the first time he'd spoken throughout the entire interview. But in his booming voice and his strained expression, I could see that he was severely disappointed by Gavin's golden boy —his first choice for the job as SEO and Content Manager.

I wanted to fight my corner. I wanted to show some willingness.

But in the end, all I could do was shake his hand and leave.

When I walked down the corridor, past the waiting trio, I saw their smiles.

And this time, as they watched me slump away, I knew those smiles weren't fake.

CHAPTER TWO

I walked into the cemetery and every instinct in my body told me just to turn around because all that waited for me here was misery.

Five days had passed since my interview, and I still hadn't heard any news, good or bad. I had been granted extended leave from work, which, as far as I saw it, pretty much confirmed that I wasn't going to be going back there anytime soon. Obviously, I was annoyed. I'd worked at that place since I was twenty-three, my first "proper" job that didn't involve washing pots or cleaning filthy toilets. I'd felt such pride when I'd gone to that place to work. Really, it filled me with confidence and kick-started my life.

I walked across the pathway, which was waterlogged. The brief stint of summer Rochdale had experienced had given way to the *usual* summer now: damp, humid, and all round a little bit depressing. As my footsteps splashed through the puddles, I saw some hoodies on bikes in the distance, hanging around the graves. It made me tighten my grip around the stalks of the flowers. It always struck me as totally disrespectful when kids hung around graveyards, a fact I'd discovered for myself as the losses in my life stacked up. I used to always tell Harriet that they were the "dregs of society," but at the time she took a much more sympathetic view. "Better hanging around with the dead than bothering the living," she'd say.

She was always so full of beautiful little turns of phrase like that. That was part of what I loved about her.

I stopped when I reached my mother's grave and I looked down at it.

Seeing her name—Patricia Harvard—etched in those capital letters was still surreal. It was hard to accept that this was all my mum was, now. Just an etching on a stone in the ground. I saw the flowers in front of her grave had all had their heads nibbled off by rabbits. And I knew the flowers I had in my hand right now would suffer the same fate.

But still, I visited, every week, just to spend some quiet time with my mum, to watch the birds circle the cemetery, listen to the silence.

I crouched beside the grave, pulled up the old flowers and snipped at the new ones before putting them in place. When I was finished, I just sat there for a while. She'd died six months ago. Heart attack, very sudden. She didn't suffer much, if at all. One second, she was with us, the next, she was gone.

There was the shock of it, of course. She was only in her late sixties, and she was a relatively healthy woman. She'd always boasted of how she'd be running long after I lost my ability to walk, teasing Harriet about her "awful posture." The pair of them got on very well, so her death came as much of a shock to Harriet as it did to me. She didn't have parents of her own. She'd been adopted, and the adoption went sour, so as far as she was concerned, my mum was the closest thing she'd ever had to a mother herself.

But we stuck together, as hard as it was. I was suddenly the man without any parents—I'd never known my dad. Harriet was my rock. She'd been by my side and I'd been by hers, right through those months of hell.

Until one evening, Harriet didn't come home from work. She walked to work, in admin and reception down at the local vets. It was a ten-minute walk, tops. She didn't have to worry about traffic or anything like that. "It's the least of my concerns," she used to say.

How ironic it was that a double-decker bus slammed into her when she was crossing the only road she had to cross every single day, breaking every bone in her body.

She didn't die instantly, though. It was all a bit of a blur, to be honest. I went out to try and find her when she wouldn't answer her calls. And when I'd seen the people gathering around, an onion I'd half-chopped still in my hand, I knew, right away, that something was wrong.

The onion fell to the road, and I fell to Harriet's side.

She was still alive, but she was gone, of course. The bus had hit her with such force that it had knocked all consciousness from her broken body.

I'd sat by the side of her hospital bed in intensive care and, even though I wasn't a religious man, I found myself praying. Not cursing God, like some people did when they lost. Just praying that Harriet wasn't going to leave me, so soon after my mum had left me.

Then my prayers changed, somehow, as if a divine hand was transforming their direction.

I was praying that whatever happened was for the best. For Harriet. For me.

I was praying that I'd find the strength to conquer whatever challenge lay ahead.

And then the doctors came in and told me the awful, life-changing news that I never thought I'd have to hear.

Harriet wasn't going to survive.

They were switching off her life support.

I glanced over in the direction of her grave. There wasn't a headstone there, yet. Just a tall wooden cross with a little gold emblem on it. There were flowers laid on the grave, but none of them mine.

I couldn't go over there.

Going over there meant acceptance that she was gone.

I still wasn't ready to accept that yet, even if it had been two months.

I tricked myself, sometimes. I listened to old voicemails she'd left me asking me to pick up tomatoes or chickpeas on the way home from work. She was a vegetarian, and yes, she'd half-converted me to her ways a few nights a week, so cooking was a favoured hobby of ours.

Other times, I read the emails she sent me when I'd been at work and pretended she'd only just sent them.

Other times... Yeah. I looked at her nudes. Shameful. Made me feel ill, simply because it was like I was attempting to resurrect her from the dead when in fact she was gone. Totally gone.

But there wasn't anything sleazy about it.

I missed her body.

I missed her skin.

I missed her warmth.

I'd never feel anything like it, ever again.

I went to stand when my phone rang, breaking me from my trance.

When I looked at the phone, I saw it was...

Shit.

Gavin.

I lifted the phone to my ear. "Gavin. All okay?"

"Hi, Scott," Gavin—my boss—said. "Look, I heard about your interview the other day."

My cheeks went red. "Ah. You did?"

"Look, I'm not gonna pretend you stormed it. But I'm not happy with the manner in which it was conducted. At the end of the day, Gregg might've bought a 70% stake in the company, but

30% of that company is still mine. I want to be there to fight my 30%."

I turned around, unable to believe what I was hearing. "Wait. Are you suggesting—"

"Congratulations, and all that," Gavin said. "Looks like you've got a second interview. But don't screw this one up. You promise me?"

"Sure," I said, my body shaking with relief. "Absolutely. I'll—I'll give it my all."

"Good," Gavin said. "Anyway. I'll leave you to it. This merger is taking it out of our systems, therefore out of me."

"Thanks, Gavin."

"Scott, it's no problem. You're a good worker and a good man. Just... be there. I'll text through the details."

"Okay. I'll see you later, Gavin."

"Oh, and Scott?"

"Yeah?"

"Do some goddamned reading up on coding. You're gonna need it."

The phone went dead.

But as I stood in the cemetery, the sun started to peek through the clouds and shone right down on Harriet's grave.

"Thank you," I muttered.

Then I hurried out of the cemetery.

I had a big night of study ahead of me.

CHAPTER THREE

Somewhere...

HE LOOKED at the weapon and he couldn't help smiling with pride when he saw it.

He'd heard about the sheer devastation a weapon like this could cause. It was attached to a nuclear warhead, which would explode above ground, rendering everything beneath it powerless. The electricity would go down. The satellites would go down. An entire country could go black.

He knew the United States had technology like this. EMP warheads, they called them. And he knew that the battle for these arms was spreading secretly and quietly around the world, unbeknownst to the general public. The general public was instead worrying about minor distractions like terrorism, immigration, the breakdown of the old world order, things like that.

They had no idea a new Cold War had been occurring right underneath their noses.

Well, they were about to find out.

He walked up to the weapon, which was surrounded by scientists in white coats. He was flanked by two of his most loyal companions. He was making sure their guidance over this project was duly rewarded.

"And you intend to launch this device, sir?"

"We must do," he said. "Before our western oppressors have the chance to hit us."

He turned around and smiled at his aide.

"Today is a great day for our nation. Tomorrow will be a day of darkness for them, and a day of prosperity for us. Are *you* ready?"

His aide smiled and nodded. "We have waited seventy years for this. Of course we are ready."

"Good," he said. Then he turned around to face the EMP warhead. "Then we begin. Line up the target. Prepare for launch. Tomorrow is the first day of the new world order. Tomorrow is the day the West dies. Tomorrow is the day we rise."

CHAPTER FOUR

I sat on the train to Manchester, still in disbelief that I'd managed to get a second interview with Holmes & Wisdom at all.

I had no idea at that point that I was on a journey that would change my life in ways I couldn't even begin to imagine.

It was eight in the morning, which meant that the train was absolutely ram-packed full of all types of people—holidaymakers going to Manchester Airport, taking up way too much corridor space with their suitcases that they didn't trust to put in the baggage areas. People in suits heading to work. Students travelling to university. It was always the case this time in the morning, which was another reason I liked the flexibility of my job—I could start at ten a.m. and stay on a little later in the evening, but honestly, Gavin used to let me leave early anyway.

I was fully aware that things were going to change under the new management. The reality was that I'd likely have to catch this crammed train every single morning, so full of people that it was warm and stuffy; a dampness of morning sweat to the compressed air, which made me feel very nauseous.

Not to mention the impending prospect of a looming interview.

I leaned back against the seat, which wasn't comfortable in the slightest. Voices rang in my ears. The train didn't seem to travel peacefully, as usual, but rocked from side to side. I didn't want to look at my watch because looking at my watch just made me face up to the reality of my situation: the train was running fifteen minutes late as it was. My interview was at nine a.m. I'd have to jog to Holmes & Wisdom from Oxford Road station, a prospect I wasn't looking forward to.

But there was no point looking at my watch anymore. That wasn't going to make time speed up. I just had to keep it together and ride this one out.

I know what you're probably thinking. A man in his early thirties living in Rochdale, which is only a twenty-minute drive from Manchester. Why not drive? Well, that's the thing. I kind of don't drive. I know, I know. I'm inept. I'm incompetent. I'm not a proper person, let alone a proper "man." But the truth was, I'd just never needed to learn to drive. I'd had a few lessons, like everyone, when I was seventeen. I was okay. But honestly, I was more interested in girls and drinking at the time, so I'd skipped a few lessons and got sacked off by my driving instructor as a result.

After that, I'd gone to university in Nottingham when I was eighteen and spent four years there studying both a BA and Masters in English with Creative Writing. When I was down there, all my jobs and all my life, for that matter, were within walking distance.

And when I finally moved up north, close to Manchester to live as affordably near to Holmes & Wisdom as I could, again, I was just a short jog from the train station. Not to mention the prevalence of Uber and public transport. Sure, having no car was a little shit in times like these, but the positives of not owning one actually outweighed the negatives, particularly from a financial perspective.

But, hell. What I'd do for a car right now.

I felt my head spinning, and when I burped, I tasted a little of my Weetabix and banana breakfast burn the back of my throat. I gulped it back, aided with a swig of water.

There was a woman sitting opposite me. She had long, brown hair, and bright blue eyes. She was pale, but attractively so, with a little freckle right in the middle of her right cheek. She was reading something on her Kindle. Or at least, she was pretending to. She seemed more interested in my sudden nauseous fit.

I swallowed back some water, and then I smiled at her. "Bit of a nightmare, this train, eh?"

She smiled back at me. "Try taking it this time every morning. I'd love to know the last time it actually got in on time."

My stomach sank, then, as I looked down at my watch. Eight fifteen. Shit. This was getting to disaster point. I usually started later, so the morning rush didn't affect me. "What, um... what time's it usually—"

I was interrupted by what I could only describe as a very sudden *halt*. It was strange. It felt like the entire train just blacked out for a split second, then sparked to life again. Over the radio, static crackled loudly.

At first, I wondered if it was just me who had been imagining things or something. But I saw the looks of the people on the train.

"My phone went. Just for a second."

"My music cut out."

All these mumbling voices, all talking about some weird kind of power cut.

I looked across the table at the woman.

She was restarting her Kindle.

She glanced up at me and rolled her eyes. "My boyfriend always says I should carry paper books with me. I guess this proves him right."

I smiled, then looked down at my watch.

Eight seventeen.

The incident before was soon forgotten as we continued our slow journey to Manchester. I started to weigh up the possibility of getting to work faster if I got off at Salford Crescent and caught a taxi, but knowing my luck, I'd just end up stuck in traffic.

I just had to close my eyes and relax. I would get there. And if I was late, I could explain. *Yeah. I'm a thirty-one-year-old man relying on someone else to drive me to work. Hire me now, yeah?*

My peaceful moment didn't last long.

I heard the sound of the train cut out, suddenly, but the train was still moving. I couldn't hear any brakes.

I saw the lights switch off inside the train.

I saw the phones go off.

I saw the woman opposite me turn her Kindle around, try to switch it on again, but to no luck.

The train was still moving, but it was gradually getting slower.

Then, I heard a massive screeching and went flying forward.

It didn't last long, but I could only assume it was some manual brake override.

And as the train came to a total halt, silence filled the carriage.

It wasn't that the train had broken down. It was the weirdness of everything else. The phones. The Kindles. Everything.

"Anyone know what the hell's going on here?" someone muttered.

And I was fascinated. Really, I was.

But naive little me was still just worried about getting to Holmes & Wisdom on time for my second interview.

I looked down at my watch, desperate to see if I had enough time left to make it from here.

The second hand had stopped.

CHAPTER FIVE

I sat totally still and waited for the train to come back to life, but that niggling voice whispering in my ear kept on telling me that something was desperately wrong.

I didn't know what time it was exactly anymore, mostly because my watch had gone, as had everyone else's in this carriage, and as had all the phones, laptops, tablets, Kindles and other e-devices. I felt totally cut off from the outside. What was even more infuriating? The fact I couldn't just call work and tell Gavin there'd been some kind of freak accident on the train and that I wasn't going to be in on time. Shit.

I was sure he'd see it on the news at some stage, though. After all, a train stuck on the line was a pretty dangerous feat. I'd seen the driver and staff stepping outside, trying to get a signal to contact some mechanics, but they seemed to be struggling too. That was surely dangerous, especially if another train was on the line.

I'd heard a few whispers and theories. Some people suggested that there must've been some kind of electrical fault on the train that was so strong it'd basically knocked out everything else in its vicinity. Others discussed more far-fetched theories—terrorist attacks, blackouts like they'd seen on television shows and movies.

Personally, I just figured I'd do as the staff said and stayed put. I wasn't going to gain anything by getting out of the train and running in the direction of Oxford Road station. I was only going to lose time—and possibly my life—by running on the tracks.

No. The train staff would get in touch with someone soon. This mechanical fault was temporary. It wasn't going to last.

It better damned not last.

"So. We're sardined on a train together. Are you going to tell me why you're so fidgety?"

I looked across the table and saw the woman with the dark hair and the blue eyes smiling at me.

I cleared my throat. "Job interview."

"Congratulations. Better luck with the next place."

"Thanks. It was a re-interview for my own job at Holmes & Wisdom Media, too. A merger. Making a good impression on the new people in charge."

"Oh," the woman said. "Yeah, that is rough. I'm sorry."

"That's okay," I said. "At least I get to spend the morning trapped on a train, without any form of electricity and surrounded by a bunch of sweaty university students."

"Living the dream," the woman said. She leaned over, held out a hand. "I'm Hannah, by the way."

"Hannah," I said, taking her hand. "I'm Scott. Nice to meet you."

"Don't lie. Neither of us wanted to meet each other in these circumstances."

I pulled my hand back, my heart pounding. To be honest, I wasn't that great at speaking to women. Well, to strangers in general, for that matter. I usually came off a little sarcastic and cutting when really I was just trying to break the ice. Misinterpretation and misunderstanding were big, big bedrocks of my existence.

But Hannah, well. She seemed to be going along with what I was saying. I appreciated her for that.

"So. What about you?" I asked.

"Me? Oh, nothing interesting. Just... well. Heading into uni."

I instantly regretted the "sweaty university students" comment. "You're at uni?"

She smirked. "Why? Do I look too old for uni or something?"

I felt my cheeks blushing. "No, it's just—"

"I'm just messing with you. Yeah, I'm at Manchester Met uni. I'm a mature student, though, as they call us. I mean, I'm thirty, but I don't feel all that mature."

"I know the feeling, sometimes. What do you study?"

"Health and social care with sociology," she said. "I kind of... well. I won't bore you with the details, but I didn't really do a lot productive in my twenties. Kinda bought into those lies that you should spend your twenties having fun, your thirties laying down the foundations for the rest of your life, and your forties settling down. Only problem is, I didn't even lay down any pre-foundations in my twenties. So it looks like the thirties is gonna be the catch-up decade."

"Well, at least you had fun in your twenties."

"You settle down the second you hit the big 2-0?"

I felt an immediate punch of regret over what I'd said. After all, my time with my wife, Harriet, were the best years of my life. I'd been happy. So ready to live like that for the rest of my life.

But now she was gone, well... I realised just how little I actually had in my life and how much I was basing all my happiness and contentment on her. I'd placed all my eggs in two baskets: a good job, and a wife that I adored.

Now both of those were gone, I'd soon realised just how easy it was for the foundations of life to tear away at the seams in two fell swoops.

"Something like that," I said. "I... I got married."

"Wow. You really did throw yourself in at the deep end, didn't you?"

"My wife. Harriet. She... she died two months ago."

I saw the jokey expression on Hannah's face drop, right then. She actually turned a little pale. "Man. I'm sorry. Genuinely."

"It's okay. You didn't know."

She wasn't so talkative after that point. I realised I should probably not have brought Harriet up. After all, bringing up the death of your wife forced a person to walk on eggshells around you and really think about what they were saying, which ultimately numbed them into not saying a thing at all.

I looked out of the window. The train staff were still investigating the train. They were still struggling with their phones. One of the women in train gear looked up at me, and I could see from her expression that she was struggling to hold the facade of normality together.

She smiled at me.

I smiled back.

And then I saw it.

I couldn't understand it at first. Honestly, it was surreal.

There was something just *falling* from the sky.

I heard a few gasps and whispers of disbelief as everyone who'd seen it realised what it was.

A helicopter. Air ambulance. Quite a way in the distance, but it was clear to see that something was very wrong.

Its rotors weren't spinning.

It was hurtling towards the ground.

It was...

"Oh sh..."

The helicopter hit the earth and exploded in a ball of fire.

Everyone looked on. Everyone inside the train, everyone outside the train, all of us transfixed by what we were witnessing.

We didn't want to say anything. None of us did.

But there was an unspoken fear amidst all of us.

A fear that what we'd just witnessed wasn't just coincidence.

A fear that the helicopter crash was possibly—possibly—related to whatever events were unfolding on this train...

That fear was about to be realised.

CHAPTER SIX

"Okay, folks. We're gonna start vacating the train right about now. We need to get off here just so we know we're..."

The train conductor didn't finish his sentence, as he stood in the middle of the carriage, looking increasingly pale by the second. But he didn't have to, not really. We all knew what he was going to say. "So we know we're safe."

And the fact that there was such an uncertainty from the people who were supposed to be looking out for you. Well... that was unsettling.

Of course, there were limitations of having somebody else responsible for where you were going, what you were doing. But there were advantages, too. And those advantages included the fact that those people in control were really in charge, no matter the situation. So when you had the conductor of the train telling you—in as many words—that he didn't know whether you were safe or not, it was time to worry.

I stood up, fast growing nauseous, not with fears of losing my job anymore of course, but with the fear that this situation was fast unraveling. I assumed we'd been stuck on this train the best part of half an hour now—I couldn't be certain of course, watchless as I and everyone else was. And in that time, as small an amount of time as it was, people were already growing frustrated and desperate for answers. If there was one thing I'd discovered in the last half an hour, it was just how attached myself and everyone else really was to the inane draw of the black mirror in our palms —the fake social media reflections of personality, the text messages with people you've never met, the snaps chronicling people's lives like it was a reality television show.

Everyone had been given a podium on the great stature of life. And that podium had collapsed, leaving everyone facing up to a terrifying fact: they were nothing more than themselves, now.

I followed the crowd of sardine-packed people out of the train. Up ahead, I could hear a couple arguing about needing to get to a hospital to see their dying father. I saw a man push another one back, as they battled to leave the train first. It was growing feral. People were reverting to base instincts. And they'd only been cut from the power for half a-bleeding-hour.

"I knew how frustrating it'd be," Hannah muttered, as we made our way to the door, which had been manually opened. "I mean, I live out in a terraced house in the countryside these days. We get power cuts all the time. Never thought of myself as one of these ultra-connected people. But hell, turn off the lights and the WiFi in a zero signal reception area, and yeah. It does get kinda refreshing. And also kinda boring."

I smirked and thought back to the time when Harriet and I had got caught in a massive power cut when we'd been staying in Center Parcs. The entire park had suffered a serious blackout, and for a while, it was disconcerting, as everyone huddled around in the darkness of the great centre.

But then we stepped outside, looked up at the beautiful stars, seeming so bright without any light pollution, and we revelled in the present moment.

Of course, that was then. This was now.

And right now, things seemed... different.

We stepped outside, and I was immediately grateful for some fresh air. Although it wasn't *that* fresh, of course. There were loads of people standing at the sides of the tracks. An old man helped an even older woman over the tracks and onto the grass at the side. I couldn't stop looking over at where that helicopter had fallen. The smoke was still rising from it. It didn't seem like anyone had seen to it yet, which I found equally bizarre.

"Looks like an EMP to me, mate. Phones down. Watches down. Transport down. End times, that's what this shit is."

I glanced to my right. There was a short, podgy lad beside me. He had long, curly ginger hair, and thick rimmed glasses. He was wearing a hoodie with Slayer written on the front, and tour dates on the back, which were fading away. It looked like he was speaking to me.

I smirked back at him, politely more than anything.

But remarkably, he didn't stop spouting his crap.

"I mean, it's possible. I read loads of subreddits on it, and on AboveTopSecret, too. EMPs. Our governments have 'em. Someone probably used one on us. Took out all the power. Or maybe a terrorist got their hands on them. Shit. I mean, if it's affected us here, then it's probably affected the whole damn country. Unless it's a solar flare. That way... shit. The whole frigging *world* could be affected."

My head was spinning with the speed this guy had been reeling theories off.

"Oh," he said, turning to me and smiling, holding out a chubby, greasy hand. "I'm Harry, by the way. But my friends call me Haz. I don't have many friends. You can call me—"

"Nice to meet you, Harry," I said, taking his hand.

He seemed part happy by the embrace of my grip, and part disappointed that I hadn't called him "Haz."

"So, genius," Hannah said, stepping towards Harry. "You're so full of theories. What do we do now?"

Harry scratched at his curly mane, dandruff falling out of it. "Well," he said. "I guess... I guess if it *is* an EMP strike, we'll know about it soon. But not through the news or anything. Just getting to Manchester and seeing if the power's down there, too."

"And how will we know if it's a solar flare or an EMP, or whatever?" Hannah asked.

Harry shrugged. "We won't. We won't ever. No one will. If the power's gone, how will we?"

I mused on the thought for a few seconds. But scary as it was, I couldn't accept what Harry was saying. It was the stuff of science fiction novels and shitty late night television shows, *not* of reality.

"Regardless of whether this is an EM-whatever or not," I said, "we'd be better off not staying around here. I take this train every day. Manchester is, what, a half an hour's walk away, if we keep up the pace? We have to get there because that's where we're all going. No point standing around here and waiting for shit to happen."

Hannah nodded. As did Harry. "Lead the way, chief navigator!" Harry said.

I didn't smile. I didn't laugh.

I just headed forward, following the small group of people already breaking off and making their way to Manchester.

I could see the buildings of the city in the distance.

I didn't know what was waiting there for me, or what to expect.

But as the smoke continued to rise from that helicopter... I couldn't help wondering.

CHAPTER SEVEN

"So, Scotty-boy. What do you do for a living?"

Twenty minutes walking alongside "Haz", as I now had no choice but to call him, and already I was exhausted.

Not from the exercise. But from Haz himself.

"I work with computers," I said.

"Whoa!" Haz shouted, so forced and exaggerated. "Computers are like, my life, bro. What kind of computer work do you do?"

I scratched the back of my neck. "Just, SEO. Marketing. That kind of thing."

Haz lowered his head as if he was disappointed by what I'd said.

"What's up?" I asked. "Not what you were expecting?"

"No, man. No problem with that. It's just... well, y'know. I thought when you said you worked in computers that you'd be working in something... well, exciting."

I smiled a little, Hannah laughed too. "Well, sorry to disappoint you. What do you do that's so exciting, anyway?"

Haz rubbed the back of his sweaty neck as we walked alongside the train line. There were small groups of people just like us walking in the same direction. There'd been no attempt to bond or join up or anything like that. After all, as far as we were concerned, we were going to get back to Manchester and find that the world was all in order.

At least, that was a dying hope that we were clinging to.

"I work on video games," Haz said.

"Video games?" I said. "Like, for kids?"

"Quiet, man. You know what the biggest age demographic is for video games?"

"Under tens."

Haz shook his head, going red and angry, which I had to admit I was enjoying. "Twenty-five to forty. Ancient, basically. Like you guys."

Hannah laughed. "Charming. I've got one man surprised I'm a uni student and another saying I'm ancient."

"Wait," Haz said, stopping. "You're a *uni* student?"

Hannah pointed a finger at him. "Don't you start, kiddo."

We kept on walking. The closer we got to the high-rise buildings of the first train station inside Manchester, the more optimistic I grew that things were all going to work out. After all, the things Haz had said about EMPs and terrorist attacks, those things—as far-fetched as they were—weren't exactly just going to go under the radar. I mean, terrorists *might, might* hypothetically attack the electrical grid for a while. But it'd get repaired.

And a solar flare, too. Sure, I'd seen a documentary or two about them happening and what they might do if they hit. But they had fail-safes in place in case of those kind of events. Those documentaries were designed to instil fear and paranoia. And from the sounds of things, Haz had soaked all that fear and paranoia right up.

"So, Hannah," Haz said. "What do you study?"

"Health and social care," Hannah said.

Haz made a mock yawn. "Damn. That sounds even more boring than Mr Computing over here—"

"Well, maybe if you took the time to put down your video game controller and actually *learned* the kind of work social care graduates do, you'd be a lot more appreciative of us."

There was a frosty silence to the air, then. Hannah had gone red. Haz was speechless. I sensed that he had really touched a sore spot. She hadn't displayed a fiery character like that since they'd started talking.

Part of me wanted to ask. Part of me wanted to inquire.

Instead, I just turned around.

"Look at that."

There was a train ahead of us. Just like ours, it had stopped on the tracks. People were getting out of it, all of them making their way towards Manchester.

"Believe me yet?" Haz said, walking around me.

I didn't. I couldn't.

We walked a little further, not saying much until eventually I saw the bridge above Manchester Oxford Road and felt a knot turn in my gut.

"Hold up," I said. "Looks like we're here."

Manchester Oxford Road station was right ahead. I could see people gathered around it from our side. But not just that. I could *hear* shouting.

But it wasn't just that.

What got me, even more, was the train on the opposite side of the track, completely abandoned.

That train had slammed right into Oxford Road station.

"Everyone evacuate!" a man shouted—whether he was police or not, I couldn't tell. Could just be a member of the public for all I knew.

We got closer to Oxford Road station. And when we got there, I realised something horrifying.

The cars on the bridge over the station had stopped. Some of them had slammed into one another. There was blood. Screaming. People trying to use phones. Chaos.

In the station itself, people were crushed inside. They were trying to climb over the ticket machines, which had broken, but were being stopped by train station staff before they could leave.

There was chaos.

There was pandemonium.

And there was one thing for sure.

"Looks like Manchester got hit too, after all," Haz said.

I didn't want to believe him.

I didn't want to accept it.

But I couldn't argue with the evidence in front of me.

CHAPTER EIGHT

It was when I stepped closer to Manchester Oxford Road train station that I realised just how bad a situation I was really engulfed in.

The sun beat down on the top of my head, burning in its intensity. I could see that the large clock dangling down in the middle had stopped right at the same time my watch and everyone else's watches and phones had stopped—eight thirty-two. All of the screens indicating train journeys had gone out. The lights in the shops had turned to nothing.

The only light came from the sun. But the sun wouldn't stick around forever. It would get to night-time eventually, and then we'd have to deal with a whole new set of problems.

No. Things would be resolved by then.

I stayed close to Hannah and Haz as we stepped back outside the train station, onto the tracks. In the station, there were a couple of trains, some of them loaded with passengers, who seemed to be taking this whole situation in their stride as if the power was just going to flick back on.

Part of me wanted to be as confident as they were. Part of me wanted to believe that this couldn't last because it just couldn't, could it? This kind of thing was the stuff of fiction. EMPs, and all that crap Haz spoke about, that wasn't rooted in real life.

Right?

I kept on telling myself there was a possibility, even the slimmest of possibilities, that everything was just going to switch back on, and we'd all put our feet up on the sofa someday and laugh about this, one day in the future.

Or more likely, we'd forget about it, just as we forgot about everything else seemingly of note at the time.

But a bigger, more omnipresent part inside me told me I wouldn't be forgetting this for a long time.

It was going to stay with me for quite a while.

"So what's the plan now?" Hannah asked, as we worked our way around the side of the train station, towards the entrance, where we'd at least be in the city and on the roads.

I thought about what we could do. I could probably still make it to work. But shit. Did I *want* to? After all, it didn't feel like this chaos was simply consigned to the train station. It felt wider spread than that. I couldn't explain why I knew that or why I felt it. But somehow I knew I wasn't the only one facing up to that reality.

"I guess... I guess we get onto the streets. Get a cab back to..."

My speech trailed off. I looked up again, at the bridge running over the station. The cars, which had slammed into each other, all of them at a halt.

"Or maybe I won't get a cab. I guess I'll—we'll have to get a hotel here or something. Until the emergency services or the army or whatever figure something out."

Haz tutted and shook his head as we made our way around to the front of the station. "Just don't get it do you, man?"

"I don't get what?"

"Emergency services. Army. You've gotta remember that all those are gonna be cut off in the same way as us. So sure, they might start trying to straighten things out. But for themselves.

On their *own* orders. If they don't answer to anyone, then we all know that isn't a good thing."

I shook my head, but I couldn't deny I was apprehensive about what Haz was saying. "They'll find a way to get things under control. I mean, you're not telling me the entire government's just going to give up their grip too, are you?"

Haz shrugged. "They might not have a choice."

We stepped around the side of the overcrowded station, where many other people were getting the same idea as us, and then we stood and looked down at the ramp leading down towards Oxford Road, Manchester.

Oxford Road was one of the busiest roads in one of the busiest cities in the UK. It was always rammed full with traffic, the sound of engines and horns honking filling the air.

Right now, there were no engine sounds.

There were no horns honking.

There were just cars, all stacked up, some of them crashed into one another.

A lot of people were in their cars, still twitching around with their phones. Others stood outside, and some even stood on their car roofs and lifted their phones to the sky, like that'd made a load of difference.

As I looked down the stretch of Oxford Road, I saw the mass of cars going back as far as I could see. The lights of electronic billboards had gone out. The city was sleeping. Or, it was dead.

But the people in it weren't.

"Believe me now?" Haz asked.

There was a little grin to his face that suggested he was somewhat happy to be living in a world like this after all... but that smile soon washed away when the reality of his predicament set in.

We walked, the three of us, zombie-like down the street. We heard men shouting at their wives. We saw people pushing one another as they argued over the positioning of their cars or the way one car had slammed into another. All of it was so feral, and I saw for definite the collective addiction to being so *connected* suffering its greatest withdrawal. Because no one was connected anymore. They were being forced to co-exist, something which the distraction of the screen and the selfie and the internet and the mass of information had relieved them of for so long.

"One thing's for sure," Hannah said, as we made our way past an office block—a block that I didn't want to tell any of them was my place of work. I looked at it. It didn't seem like there was anyone in there. The place was dead. My hopes of getting my job, dead.

"And what's that?" I asked, with a sigh.

She lifted her Kindle out of her pocket. "I should've listened to my boyfriend when he told me to carry a paper book with me."

She smiled. I smiled back. Haz smiled, too.

The smiles were soon broken when we heard a scream coming from my workplace.

CHAPTER NINE

I heard the scream coming from inside the offices of my workplace and I knew I couldn't just stand around.

"I'm guessing you heard that?" Haz said. "And it wasn't just, like, me hallucinating or something?"

"No, I heard it," I said. I walked towards the steps of Holmes & Wisdom. I could see that folders and papers had been dropped, obviously in a hurry to get out of there. I looked at the car park around the side. Some people that I recognised were in their cars. Others, nowhere to be seen.

Those others included Gavin, my old boss.

I hoped, wherever he was, that he was okay.

The scream echoed out again.

"Help us! Somebody help us!"

"We can't just stand around here," Hannah said, stepping in front of me.

"Wait," I said, holding her hand to pull her back, something she immediately broke free of. "Sorry. It's just... it could be dangerous in there."

"So, what? We're supposed to just ignore this, are we? Damn, Scott. You must hold a real disdain for your work colleagues."

I felt my cheeks blushing then. Shit. She'd remembered where I said I worked. "I'm just trying to be rational, that's all."

"Rational doesn't include ignoring screaming people. Haz. Are you with me?"

Haz rubbed the back of his neck and looked over his shoulder like he hadn't heard Hannah.

"I'll take that as a no."

"I'll just, um, keep watch out here. Okay?"

"Coward."

"What?"

"Scott. Are you with me?"

I looked up at Holmes & Wisdom. Hannah was right. I couldn't just ignore a scream, especially when it was from someone I probably knew. But that was part of my fear, here. Coming across someone I knew, someone I liked, in a horrible situation. The possibilities of why someone would be screaming spun around my mind. The electricity had gone. Maybe there'd been some kind of power surge. A surge that had killed people...

I didn't know. I couldn't be sure.

I just had to get inside and find out for myself.

"Come on," I said, walking past Hannah and leading the way.

"Good," she said. "Glad you've come to your senses. Haz?"

Haz shook his head. He looked uncomfortable about all this, to say the least. "Like I said. I'll keep watch."

Hannah sighed. "You do that. Wimp."

"What?"

"Nothing!"

Hannah and I stepped through the doors of my Holmes & Wisdom offices. They were automatic, but the glass had been smashed from the inside, summing up the desperation of whoever was inside to get out, for whatever reason. As I crunched over the broken glass, I questioned whether I could really believe that society would revert to such a state in such a short space of time.

I looked over my shoulder onto the car-packed road, listening to the arguments, the frustration, all bubbling over the surface... yeah, I could believe it.

Humanity was rearing its ugly head. I wasn't sure it would ever be able to cover itself up again, not even if the power came back.

When the power came back.

I looked around the reception area. The desk had been vacated. A couple of phones had been left behind. I lifted them, checking them just in case, but they were down completely. Just as expected.

The clock was stuck at eight thirty-two, just like my watch, just like every other timepiece.

The scream echoed through the building again. It came from the right.

"We're in the lift! Someone, please! We can't get out!"

My stomach sank, then. I thought I vaguely recognised the voice, but I couldn't be certain to who it belonged.

But they were in the lift. Of course they were. Trapped in an elevator when the power had gone out. I couldn't think of many things more terrifying.

"It's okay!" Hannah called. "We're here! We're coming for you!"

Silence, as we stood in front of the heavy metal doors of the lift.

Then, "Okay. Oh, thank God. I thought we were going to be in here forever."

"Where's the lift shaft?" Hannah asked.

"The lift shaft?"

"You know. Like you see on films. There's always a way of getting into the lift shaft and, like, opening a little hatch on top of it, isn't there?"

"I... well. On films, maybe."

"You're saying you don't know where your workplace's lift shaft is?"

"Oh, I'm sorry. The next time I get hired, I'll remember to make a careful note of where the nearest lift shaft is."

Hannah shook her head. "Let's try the stairs."

We made our way up, searching for some way into the lift. In the end, we were led right up to the roof.

When we stood on it, we looked out over the city. The sun was high, now. It seemed brighter than I was used to seeing it. There was a light breeze in the air.

But the scene in front of me was well and truly staggering.

The entire city, as far as I could see, was at a gridlock.

People were standing on top of buildings opposite, just like me.

Holding their phones into the air.

Losing their minds.

Everyone so disconnected.

Everyone on their own.

And when I saw that sight, I realised for the first time—despite everything I'd seen already—that this was the world now. The power was gone. I didn't know how far this blackout stretched, but it was happening in central Manchester, and as far as I knew, it could be happening elsewhere, too.

I saw lines in the sky, where planes had spiralled out of control. I could only think of the devastation of all the many passenger jets flying through the sky, suddenly losing the ability to stay in the air.

I knew some pilots would still be able to land those planes, steering them to safety.

But most of them wouldn't. There would only be so much space on runways and open fields.

Most of the planes would slam into the earth, taking people on the ground out as well as the people on board.

"Scott?" Hannah said.

I turned around. She was standing by an open door.

"Looks like I found the hatch," she said.

I walked over to it. It was quite a drop down. There was a metal ladder-like grip on the side running down it.

"After you?" she said.

I felt fear grip hold of me as I held onto the rusty old climbing ladders and made my way down the hatch. "Much appreciated."

The further down I got into this dark, damp hatch, the more I longed for the light of above. What if I fell? What if the elevator came back to life and shot up towards me? Was that even possible?

As I considered these scenarios, I realised just how little I actually knew about electricity myself, and the way the world worked. Sure, I could criticise people for naively poking their phones into the air. But was I much better, much more qualified or adept, really?

I reached the top of the elevator, and I gripped its sides.

With some force, I yanked it open.

When I opened it, I saw one unfamiliar face looking back at me, and one familiar face, too.

I helped the man out. He was a muscular black guy who was here to work on the IT systems, apparently. His name was Remy. He seemed a nice enough guy, but the irony of him here to work on IT on the day IT became obsolete was certainly lost on him.

The second person—the woman—I recognised.

The last time I'd seen her, she'd made my interview hell.

"Scott?" she said. With relief or disappointment, I wasn't sure.

"Julia. Pleasure to see you again."

She gave me that same condescending smile she'd given me back in my first interview, and I helped her out of the elevator.

When we got out, we filled the pair of them in on what had happened to us. Haz made his way up to the roof now we were sure it was safe.

We looked out at the city, me, Hannah, Haz, Remy, and Julia. All of us were silent. All of us were absorbing what we were looking at, what we had to face.

"If it's global..." Haz started. Then he stopped. His morbid curiosity seemed to have changed to a genuine fear.

But I couldn't shoot down his fear anymore. I could only feel it, just like he did.

"What do we do?" Julia asked.

I took a deep breath as the shouts and cries of the city echoed around me.

"We have to get out of this city," I said. "And we have to find out just how widespread this blackout really is. Fast."

CHAPTER TEN

I walked with Hannah, Haz, Remy, and Julia as we tried to figure out where the hell we were going to go next.

We decided to get away from Oxford Road, for a start. That place was no fun for anyone. The rest of the roads weren't much better, in fairness. There were cars abandoned, some of them in the middle of the road, others just on the edges of driveways. However, there were also a lot of people still sitting in their cars, waiting. Others were struggling with their phones.

"Some of these people won't even know how widespread it is," Haz said. "That's the scary thing. They don't have any news. As far as they're concerned, they're just having a rough day. They have no idea."

"We have to take advantage of that," Hannah said.

I turned to her. I was surprised by how direct and assertive she was being, especially after we'd only all recently agreed that this really was as serious a situation as Haz was suggesting.

"And how do we do that?" Remy asked. He was mostly silent, but he seemed like a good guy. Like me, he was sceptical about this blackout, at least initially. But he was growing in certainty that something terrible and disastrous had happened the further we walked into the suburbs, and the more he saw just how much things had gone to shit.

"I'd say the first thing we do is get to a store," Hannah said. "If we're going to be walking, we need some water, and some food for that matter."

"Better be quick," Haz grunted. "As soon as people realise this isn't just a momentary blip, they're gonna be straight in those stores salvaging everything they can. It's gonna be ugly."

Julia frowned. "How do you know all of this?"

Haz smiled. "Television and video games, mostly." He sideglanced at me and Hannah. "You know. Those things for ten-year-olds."

Expectedly, Julia didn't see the funny side.

"There's a convenience store a few streets down," I said. "It's not the biggest place. One of these express shops. But it's not in such a busy area. I reckon we'll be able to pick up a few things on our way."

"Maybe the power will be back by the time we get there," Julia said, optimistically.

I tilted my head to one side. As much as I didn't like Julia— and I had good reason not to—I had to sympathise with her naivety. I didn't want to face up to the task at hand, either. I knew we were going to encounter some awful things; things we wanted to forget. I didn't know how long this blackout was going to last.

But I knew, for sure, that the government, the police, the army... they weren't in control.

We'd seen a few police officers back at Oxford Road. They were on foot, trying to restore order within the crowd. Fights had broken out, as the battle for information—humanity's addiction—spilled over. Not just amongst the crowds, but the police, too.

I knew that it would only get worse if the problem weren't resolved soon. The riot police would come in. Maybe the army would come in. There would be a struggle for power, none of it sanctioned by the government.

Or maybe hope would prevail.

Maybe, just maybe, humanity wouldn't go the way of the movies but would actually find a way to be strong and pull together in the face of adversity.

I smiled. "Yeah, right."

"What was that?" Julia asked.

I looked to my left, realising I'd spoken aloud, and also realising I was walking just with Julia. Remy was just ahead of us, and Hannah and Haz were leading the way.

I shook my head. "Nothing."

"I swear you spoke."

"Just thinking aloud. Let's get to the shop."

"Scott," Julia said. "I..."

I looked around at her, and for a moment, I thought she was actually going to say the words she'd owed me for so long.

Then she took a deep breath and carried on walking. She didn't say another word.

I didn't hate many people, but I hated Julia.

What she'd done when I was suffering through my mother's death.

What she'd done when Harriet was hit by that car.

The lack of compassion she'd shown. The sheer disdain for another human.

I couldn't ever forgive her for that.

And now I was stuck with her.

We reached the shop a few minutes later. There were a couple of people inside, all of them scrambling to fill their baskets and trolleys with water, the last of the fresh meats, tins, things like that.

"So, Haz," I said. "Any idea of an ideal post-apocalyptic shopping list?"

Haz smirked. "What do you think? Follow me."

We made our way to the cheese counter, where Haz took a few kinds of cheeses with skins on—they would stay fresh for a while, he insisted. We also took plenty of peanut butter, for protein, and Haz grabbed a couple of rucksacks and a few bits and bobs that I didn't really get a chance to look at, too. Of the things I did notice, there was everything from protein bars to metal cooking pots to water bottles to first aid kits and travel towels. He really seemed to know what he was looking for.

"It's impressive, you know?" I said.

Haz frowned. "What is?"

"Your knowledge for all this stuff. Fair play, kid. I thought you were an annoying shit when we first met. Now, you're growing on me."

Haz smiled. It was the warmest, most genuine smile I'd seen from him. His eyes actually lit up as if the approval had sparked something inside him. "Thanks, Scotty-b—"

"Call me Scotty-boy and we're through," I said.

We walked around the aisle where the bottled water and other drinks were stacked. I grabbed a coke, which Remy took from me and put back on the shelf.

"Feel free to drink that crap," he said, "but don't be asking for any of my water when you get dehydrated."

I sighed and took a bottle of water. Boring old water.

When our baskets were filled, we made our way to the counter.

Only there was a problem.

The shopkeeper was holding a baseball bat, shaking his head.

"What—"

"No take my stuff. No take my stuff!"

"Hey," I said, scrambling for my wallet. "We'll pay—"

"No take my stuff!"

He swung the baseball bat towards me.

I ducked just out of its way in time. When I was down, I saw two options opening up. Stay here and try to talk this man into letting us take this stuff.

Or run away. Leave.

Steal the stuff.

Our first crime.

I'd never stolen a thing in my life. I wasn't ready for this.

"Scott!" Haz shouted, pouring the contents of the basket into one of the rucksacks. "We need to get outta this place!"

"No leave! No go nowhere!"

The man swung that bat a few more times. It was clear to me now that he was realising just how serious the goings-on were and that he was planning on battening down the hatches and keeping everything for himself.

But I couldn't let him do that.

We couldn't let him do that.

"I'm sorry," I said, as we stood by the door, the shopkeeper running towards us, baseball bat in hand.

I threw thirty pounds out of my wallet towards him.

Then, I slammed the door in his face, and, basket of shopping in hand, I ran.

CHAPTER ELEVEN

"If we *are* going to get anywhere," Haz said, "it's time we started actually thinking about *how* we're going to get around."

I heard what Haz was saying, as I looked over my shoulder back down at Moss Side, where we'd just run from the shop owner who'd chased us with a baseball bat. I was gasping and had a nasty stitch right through the left side of my body. It sure showed just how unfit I actually was, which was never a good thing to suddenly discover in a world where fitness was going to be pretty paramount.

We sat together, me, Haz, Hannah, Remy, and Julia, all of us holding on to our shopping baskets. Haz was loading up the rucksacks with the things we'd grabbed from the store.

Julia's eyes were wide, and her face was pale. "I... I can't believe we just *stole* this stuff."

"We didn't steal it," Haz said. "Scott threw him a few notes. Right?"

Julia shook her head. "No. This is wrong. We—we should take it back."

"Julia," Hannah said, clearly losing her patience with Julia as well, now. "That shopkeeper just chased us with a baseball bat. If there was any order in the world, you should see by now that it has gone."

She put her head in her hands. "I just... I just want to go home."

Hannah looked at me, then half-smiled. She patted Julia on her back. "And you probably will get home soon. But for now, we have to—"

"Quiet," Haz said.

Julia didn't hear Haz out. "My husband. He—he always cooks fish on a Wednesday. The most delicious salmon and sweet potato dish. I—I can't be late for him."

"Even if he wanted to cook salmon," I said, "he couldn't. The power's out."

"I bet you're loving this, aren't you?" Julia snapped.

"Guys," Haz said.

I narrowed my eyes at Julia. "What?"

"All this time, you've been waiting for a chance to get back at me. Well, here it is, Scott. Here's your chance to see me in tears. Savour it."

I wanted to hold back, but I couldn't. My blood was boiling with what Julia just said. "This isn't all about me and you, Julia," I said. "This isn't some selfish revenge mission of mine. This is real life. And in case you haven't noticed, it's in the shit."

"Guys!" Haz said.

"So unless you—"

Right then, someone covered my mouth.

It took me a few seconds to realise it was Remy.

I looked where Remy was looking and realised Haz was looking there too. So too was Hannah, and now Julia was, as well.

I didn't register what they were looking at initially.

But then I saw it.

There was a group of five. All of them were kitted up in cycling gear. They were standing outside an ATM, struggling to get it to work. One of them was looking at his pedometer, tapping at it.

Their bikes were a few metres away, leaning against the wall of the building.

"You know what we have to do," Haz said.

He didn't have to explain what he meant to me. I knew exactly what he wanted us to do. It was hard to face up to what he was suggesting. After all, it was wrong—morally bankrupt, in fact.

"We're supposed to just *steal* the bikes?" Hannah said.

"Oh God," Julia said. "Oh God, I'm going to be sick."

"Look," Haz said, speaking more assertively now. "I know it's not nice. It's not right, even. But if we want to get to the next town and see what's really going on here, then our best chance is by bike."

"I'm not a thief," Julia said. "I won't be a part of this."

"Then stay," I said.

My voice was louder than I'd intended. We didn't want to draw the attention of the cyclists our way. But it was loud enough to get the point across.

"Look," I said. "I... I don't like this either. But right now, I can't see what else we can do."

Julia scoffed. "I always knew you were corrupt."

"Whatever we do," Hannah cut in, "we can't just sit around here and argue. We have to make a call. Right now."

We all looked at one another. Haz was clearly in. I'd put myself in the hat, as uncomfortable I was about all this, too.

When I nodded, so too did Hannah. Remy sighed and nodded too just moments later.

So it was just Julia left.

She was crying. Shaking her head.

"It's just a temporary thing," I said. "Just while we figure out what's going on. It doesn't make us criminals."

"Then what will?" Julia said.

In that space of a second, I thought of the things I'd done

already today—stolen from a shop, and now considered stealing bikes—and I wondered just how far I would go, after all.

"Oh. Shit. Now's our chance."

Haz stood, and I saw why right away.

The cyclists were walking into the bank.

Their bikes were still by the side of the building.

"Now!" Haz said.

We ran down the side of the hill. And as we did, I couldn't shake the adrenaline I felt. This didn't feel real. And maybe that was the way to approach it. Don't *let* it feel too real. Make it just pretend. Like you're playing.

We got to the bikes. I climbed on top of one of them. I could hear the voices of the cyclists just metres away.

Remy climbed on his. Then Hannah, and Haz, then Julia, struggling to balance.

"Come on," Haz said, "we have to cycle away before they—"

"Hey!"

The shout made my body turn to stone.

The cyclists were outside of the bank. They were looking right at us.

"These bastards are stealing our bikes!"

In that split second, I had a choice. Explain myself. Try to figure out a solution. That was the sensible thing to do; the *right* thing to do.

But in the end, I knew what the survivor's thing to do was.

"Let's go," I said.

Haz cycled clear of two of the cyclists, shooting off up the road. Remy was next, manoeuvring around them before they could get a grip.

Then Hannah followed, and one of the cyclists reached for the wheel of the bike.

I kicked their hand away before they could grab her, and my tire went over their fingers, to a yelp of pain.

I picked up my speed, then, Hannah by my side. I still

couldn't believe what I'd just done. Not only had I *stolen* a bike, but I'd just done something constituting an assault. A mugging.

God help us if the power came back.

Suddenly, I heard a thump.

Then, right behind us, I heard a cry.

When I looked over my shoulder, I realised what was happening.

Julia was on the road. She'd fallen off her bike. One of the cyclists was by her side, standing over her, then another pulled her to her feet and restrained her, saying something about police and citizen's arrest.

"Help me," she called, making eye contact with me. "Scott. Please. Don't leave me here. Don't leave me!"

I wanted to go back. I wanted to help. And I saw the expression on the faces of the cyclists—they half-expected us to turn around and head back, too.

"What do we do?" Hannah asked.

I gritted my teeth together and looked back at the woman I'd hated for so long, and I couldn't help pitying her.

"We go," I said, leaving Julia behind and peddling off into the distance.

CHAPTER TWELVE

We cycled for the best part of an hour, but we didn't make as much progress as I'd have liked.

The problem was, in a world where every single car seemed to have broken down, bikes were suddenly a very valuable commodity. And I saw it in the eyes of the strangers we cycled past. They stood at the side of their cars, phones to their ears in an attempt to bring some semblance of communication back to life, and they looked at me, Hannah, Haz, and Remy with envy. There was a lack of acceptance there, too. A determination not to leave their cars, because leaving their cars meant accepting that the world had changed in such a short space of time.

In that sense, we were one step ahead.

I just wasn't sure I was quite ready to face up to the road ahead—however long it stretched on—yet.

I looked at the others ahead of me, and I couldn't help feeling guilty about what had happened back at the bank, where we'd taken the bikes. Julia had got left behind. We could've gone back for her. Don't get me wrong—I didn't like the woman, after everything she'd done to me. But I still didn't like the idea that she was going to be as good as alone in this world from now on, at least until the power came back on.

But if it didn't...

I shuddered. I couldn't think like that.

"So. What was with you two back there?"

I narrowed my eyes, surprised to hear a voice. When I looked to my left, I saw it was Hannah.

"What do you mean?"

"Don't lie to me," Hannah said, stopping cycling and taking a large swig of water—something which Haz shouted at her for, telling her she was going to need all the water she could get. "I could see the way you two were with each other. Ex-lovers or something?"

"Oh, God no. Me and Julia? God no."

"Then what was with the animosity?"

"Does it matter?"

"Well. We might be stuck with each other for a while. It'd help to know you aren't really some misogynistic psycho who's gonna turn on me eventually, too."

I shook my head. "Look. Where I worked. I'd been there for eight years. But... but around the time Harriet died, a higher position became available. Like, a wider manager, with more responsibilities than just the SEO and marketing side of things. I was in a good position for that promotion, and the whole work thing gave me something to focus on, really. I'd served there the longest. I knew my stuff. I was ready for the leap."

"And she shanked you?"

"Not just shanked me," I said, fast growing uncomfortable. "She framed me."

"Wait, what?"

"She accused me of stealing company money. Made it look like I had."

"Shit. While you were grieving, too? That's pretty crappy. And you survived at that place, somehow?"

"Only reason I survived is 'cause I had a good guy fighting my corner. In the end, I still had to accept responsibility for what I'd done, on the advice of lawyers. But as you can imagine, after that, I wasn't really friends with many people there. At least, not the older blood, anyway. And to have Julia a position above me all that time, too... salt in the wounds."

"Phew," Hannah said. "To be fair, that does sound like a legitimate reason to hate."

We started cycling again, slowly this time. Fingers crossed, we'd be out of Manchester soon and into one of the many surrounding towns to monitor the situation. "So what about you?" I asked.

Hannah pretended she hadn't heard me. I could tell it was pretend. "Hmm?"

"You are full of questions and curiosities about me. But all I know about you is you're a mature university student studying health and social care, and that you have a boyfriend."

Hannah lowered her head then. "It doesn't really matter about me, does it?"

"No, I just thought—"

"There's not a lot to know. I'm just getting by in life. Until this frigging EMP—or whatever Haz calls it—hit anyway."

I wanted to press Hannah even further for information on her past. But I took her sudden misdirection as a cue to be silent, not to push her any more. I'd already seen her snap at Haz when he criticised what she was studying. I didn't know why that was, but I knew he must've hit a sore spot, and it only made me more curious about why she'd be so defensive.

But now wasn't the time, and now wasn't the place. I knew that.

It was just me and three other total strangers, all of us doing our best to get by.

"Shit," Remy said. He stopped, as did Haz. "You seen this?"

Up ahead, I saw the outline of a hospital building. The car

park was a disaster zone. Ambulances had slammed into the sides of cars. Some had toppled right over.

By the sides of the ambulances, there were ambulance workers and paramedics trying to reassure people lying on trolleys that everything was going to be okay.

Others were shaking their heads and covering the bodies of the newly deceased.

I couldn't see properly inside the hospital, and I knew it would be unwise to get too close. But I could see small flickers of movement, and I didn't need a vivid description to figure out exactly what was going on.

But Haz decided to give me one anyway.

"Think of all the life support machines. People, dead, in an instant. Think of all the people under anaesthetic for emergency surgery, and even non-emergency surgery. Think of all the chemists that can no longer deliver prescriptions. And... shit. Just think of all the people who've *tried* to call emergency services since shit went down, and how many haven't got through."

It painted a grim picture. A very morbid picture. And perhaps above anything, it rammed home the severity of the situation more than anything I'd experienced thus far.

This wasn't just any ordinary blackout.

This wasn't just something they could switch back on.

This was people, dying.

"Come on," Remy said, cycling off into the distance. "We should go."

I took a deep breath as I saw the flickers of pandemonium behind the hospital windows, as I saw another man get a white sheet spread over his body on one of those trolleys, and then I cycled away.

It might've been bad.

But I had no idea the worst was yet to come.

CHAPTER THIRTEEN

It was an hour later that we came across the first real thing that threatened our lives.

The sun was lowering, which meant it must be early afternoon. It was strange, having something of a track of time, without actually, really knowing what time it was. At least it was sunny, Hannah kept saying—like that made a load of difference. To be honest, I wasn't sure if she really believed what she was saying. Her words sounded a little... well, forced. And this whole optimistic vibe that was coming from her was at odds with the rest of her character, as I'd experienced so far.

We should've seen the tunnel coming from a long way away. The cars started racking up on the road beside us. We were out of Manchester now, but that didn't mean our surroundings were really any less urban.

Then we reached the tunnel and knew there was only one way we could go.

"So," Remy said. "If we can't go over it... if we can't go around it, there's only one way we *can* go, right?"

Remy was fast becoming the voice of reason, even though I didn't—and nobody did—know a thing about him. He was quiet, but when he did speak, it was reassuring and to the point. And after Hannah's display about not wanting to reveal much about herself, I couldn't exactly start probing at Remy, especially not now.

"There must be another way," Hannah said.

"Back," Haz said. "Far away from here."

Remy shook his head. "This is the best route. The most direct route."

"But we know what it's going to be like down there," Hannah said.

"We don't know that for certain," Remy said. "I mean, these cars here. Some abandoned. Others... no real fuss around them. Trust me. The second people get trapped in a tunnel, they aren't just gonna stay there."

I saw them looking at me like they wanted *me* to make a decisive decision. I wasn't used to being placed in that position. After all, I'd been stabbed in the back the last time I'd tried to reach a leadership role at work.

But these people were looking at me now, and I knew I couldn't just stand by. I had to step in and make my voice a part of the crowd of many voices.

"I think... I think maybe Remy's right."

Hannah sighed. Haz looked mortified.

"You realise that if anything happens to these bikes," Hannah said, "it's on you. Right?"

"Right," I said, although it was more out of pettiness than simply accepting full responsibility for my actions. I wasn't willing to accept sole responsibility for this. I was just making a decision based on what seemed like the best option, just like the rest of these people here were.

"Then we'd better make a move," Hannah said. "We'd better get this done with. Fast."

"Guys, I'm not sure about this," Haz said.

I sighed. I might've expected that. "Then don't come."

"No. That's not fair. I mean, you... you need me."

Hannah smirked. "We *need* you, do we?"

"If it weren't for me, you wouldn't even be on bikes right now. You wouldn't have your backpacks packed full of stuff that'll keep you alive. And if it weren't for me, right now you wouldn't even have a clue what was going on."

"Your theory is still only a theory," I said.

"Yes, but it's the best damned theory you've got."

"Guys," Remy said.

"I'm just saying," Haz continued. "If we want to make a collective decision here, it has to be collective. And I'm a part of that collective."

"Guys!"

Remy's voice broke through the rest of the conversation. When we heard it, we turned around, because there was a reminder in his tone of the way Haz had spoken when he was trying to get our attention about the bikes a few miles back.

This time, though, as I held my breath, there weren't the crowds I expected. There weren't people like the scavengers. Or worse, people trying to scavenge our bikes and our equipment.

When I saw what Remy was bringing our attention to, the realisation was subtle, at first.

And then it clicked.

There was a movement up ahead, right in front of the tunnels.

It was coming from one of the cars. A red Honda Civic, which had smashed into a green Toyota Prius.

That movement was a person's arm.

"Shit," I said.

There was someone trapped between the cars. I could see blood rolling down their raised arm, which flailed weakly.

"They might not have long left," Remy said. "We need to check on them."

"No way," Haz said.

I turned to him, head on. "What is your problem?"

"It's—it's too dangerous down there. This might be some kind of trap."

"Oh, wake up from your little fantasy," Remy cut in, more direct and agitated than I'd seen him up to now. "There's someone down there who needs our help. And we're supposed to just stand by?"

"Then you go," Haz said. His voice was shaky, and there were visible tears rolling down his cheek. "I'll wait here and—"

I didn't hear what Haz said next. I saw the surprise on the faces of Remy, Hannah, and Haz too, but mostly I heard a ringing in my ears and felt a suffocating pain split through my skull.

I fell off my bike, slammed against the road.

My vision was blurry. I didn't realise what had happened, not at first.

But when I saw the movement—movement not from Remy, or Hannah, or Haz—but movement from someone else, I knew what had happened.

"Just let me take it and I'll leave you alone," a voice said, muffled, mumbled.

And then I saw them lifting my bike and taking off with it.

But more than that.

I saw more people emerging from their cars. Ones who'd just been sitting in there, watching as the world went by.

They were looking at us like they had an idea, now.

Looking with a feral gaze in their eyes. Like they had got an idea from the man who'd stolen my bike that yes, travelling by bike was the best option right now.

There were four people. Four men, for that matter. All of them were standing outside their car. All of them were looking at us. Me, Hannah, Remy, and Haz.

All of them wanted the rest of our bikes.

"What do we do now?" Haz asked, fear in his voice.

I looked down towards the tunnel, and I knew we had no choice now. "We run."

CHAPTER FOURTEEN

I wasn't sure I'd ever really felt real, undiluted adrenaline before this point in my life.

I raced down towards the entrance of the tunnel. My head was spinning and aching after the blow I'd taken to it. I could feel something warm and sticky trickling down the side of it, and I knew that it was blood.

I looked over my shoulder and fast realised that I was leading the way now after all. The four men who had been pursuing us were down to three, as one had managed to take Haz's bike. Judging by the way Haz was running, he wasn't all too fussed that he'd lost his bike. He just wanted to get away.

Remy and Hannah, however, were holding onto their bikes for dear life. But it was rapidly becoming clear that we were heading in one direction, and that direction wasn't exactly the most comfortable one.

Whether we liked it or not, we were heading into the tunnel.

Into the mouth of the beast.

But as we ran towards it, mingled amidst all the fear and terror I felt, there was something strange. And that something strange brought a smile to my face. It felt like, for the first time in many years, I was back to my childhood again. Back to pretending to be running away from some perceived threat, even though in the back of my mind I was loving every second of it.

That said, this wasn't just some perceived threat now. It was a real threat.

But the child in my mind was having the biggest blast since... well, since childhood.

I felt a stitch tearing at my stomach and realised just how unhealthy I was, how unhealthy I'd become. Not that I didn't eat well. I cooked good food. But exercise, despite not being able to drive a car, was something that didn't come easily for me.

Shit. At least I was going to get plenty of it in this new world.

I heard a crash, and when I looked back, I saw that Hannah had given up her bike now, too, and was sprinting towards me, and towards the entrance of the tunnel. Remy was the only one holding on, and he was lagging. Just two men were chasing him. He almost had this.

Then everything went dark.

I didn't know why. Not at first. But then it dawned on me that we were in the tunnel now.

I saw the mass of cars. I heard screams in the distance. I could smell fumes. Shit. This was dangerous. The collisions could had started a fire. This was a bad idea. It was always going to be a bad idea. Why had I ever thought this was a good idea? This world wasn't for me.

I looked to my right, then, and I realised this was the point where I'd seen the arm waving from a distance, splattered in blood.

That arm had stopped waving now.

It had given up.

I'd failed.

Then, a final crash and Remy was running along with us, bike free.

We stopped, then. Stopped, just in the mouth of the tunnel.

Over our shoulder, the men who had been chasing us weren't interested in us anymore. They were busier scrapping with each other over the new ownership of the bike.

I didn't plan to get involved. Not anytime soon.

"So we're bike-free. What now?"

Remy sighed. "We make our way through here. Slowly. Steadily."

"Even with the burning?" I asked.

"We wanted to get to Salford. This is our best chance."

I felt the adrenaline being taken over by nerves, and I tensed my fists together.

"Looks like it's our only hope. Wait… Haz? Haz, what the…"

When I looked at Haz, I felt the biggest dose of horror I'd experienced yet, in spite of all of the strange things I'd witnessed.

Haz was on the ground. He was curled up in a tearful, gasping ball. He was shaking badly.

"Is he…"

"My heart," he mumbled. "My—my heart."

"Shit," I said. "I think he's having a heart attack."

I went to sit down beside him, not that I knew any first aid to help him with.

But before I could get to his side, Remy pushed me out of the way and turned Haz onto his back, then gently lifted him so he was sitting upright.

"Haz, I want you to breathe for me."

"I can't."

"Deep breath in through the nose. Hold it for a second, then deep breath out, through the mouth."

"I can't—I—"

"Yes, you can. Come on. Deep breath in."

Haz attempted it.

"Deep breath out. Good, Haz. Good. Now keep going like that. Come on. In, out. In, out."

Soon, Haz was in control of his breathing. He'd stopped

clutching his chest. The colour had returned to his cheeks, and he seemed a lot calmer.

It was then that I realised Remy was more medically trained than maybe I'd have given him credit for—and certainly more medically adept than I was.

"Is he—"

"Panic attack," Remy muttered.

"But he said his heart was—"

"Trust me. It was a panic attack."

He cleared his throat, took a few methodical breaths of his own, and then turned to face us. "We should move. Right now. The tunnel's not a long one. There'll be far longer and more dangerous ones than this. We're lucky, in that sense. Now we don't have our bikes anymore, so climbing over the fences at the side of this tunnel is possible. But this is the best, most direct route, and will get us to Salford quickest."

There was a pause, then. And in that pause, weirdly, I knew—and I figured everyone knew—what Remy was about to say.

"But chances are, if it's like what it's like here, then it's gonna be like this in Salford too."

"I told you," Haz said, sounding more in control now. "This thing. This EMP. It's got the whole damned country. Maybe even the whole damned world."

I couldn't agree. But I couldn't argue, either.

I just had to fall in line, taking a back seat and following, like I always had.

"So what now?" I asked.

Another pause. Then, "I think it's about time we started thinking about self-preservation," Remy said.

"Self-preservation?" Hannah asked.

"We've got a few supplies, but not enough. It's time we started going to the nearest supermarkets. Gathering whatever we can. Because that stuff's only gonna be there once. And when it's gone... it's gone."

The thought of supermarkets running out of food and water and all kinds of supplies was a haunting one.

But Remy was right.

We had to make a move on the supermarkets, while we still could.

We had to scavenge, while there were still things to scavenge.

"Ready?" he asked.

Hannah nodded.

I looked at Haz. I put a hand on his shoulder. He flinched, then seemed to return to the present moment.

"Ready?" I echoed to him.

"Ready," Haz said.

I took a deep breath, steadied my breathing—just the way Remy had told Haz to steady his—and then I walked down into the tunnel, Hannah, Haz, and Remy by my side, and towards what might well turn out to be the final shopping trip of my life.

CHAPTER FIFTEEN

When we stepped out of the tunnel, we were different people to the ones who stepped in.

The sun was lower, and there was a warmth to the air that did no good to cool us down. I was covered in sweat, the smell of smoke filling my nostrils. I felt like I'd been forced through some kind of haunted house of horrors. I didn't want to face up to the things I'd seen, even in the pitch blackness. I was doing my best to push them from my mind already.

We had been walking for another half hour or so. Obviously, I couldn't be certain of the *exact* times. As we headed down the edge of the road, we passed by more and more people who were asking if we were having the same problems, things like that. We tried to look just as confused and as baffled as everyone. In a sense, we were, really. We had no advance knowledge. Haz's theory was still admittedly just a theory.

But it was clear that his theory was correct, or close to correct.

The confusion was growing increasingly widespread by the second.

"You guys got any signal?" a woman asked, as we passed by her Toyota Corolla.

"None," I muttered.

She scratched her head, clearly looking like she was struggling. "My daughter. She... she needs her medication. Shit. Shit."

I felt total sympathy for this woman. I wished I could help her, and her daughter. But there was nothing I could do.

All I could do was be honest.

"If I can tell you what I think's going on," I said. "I... I don't know when the electricity is coming back. I don't know if it ever will. So if you need some medication, you might want to think about walking over to wherever you're heading. And you might want to think about gathering as much of that medication as possible."

"But what if it runs out?" she gasped. "What if there's none left?"

I saw the desperation in her eyes, but there was nothing I could give her in return. "I'm sorry," I said. "I'm so sorry."

We walked on. In the distance, I could see the supermarket.

"Ah, hell," Remy said.

I didn't know what he was "ah hell"ing about. Not at first.

Then I saw the lines of people swarming through the car park and into the supermarket.

"It's begun," Haz said. He probably meant for it to sound grand and haunting, but instead, he just ended up sounding very, very afraid.

"We still go in there," I said. "Right?"

Remy shrugged. "We do what we can to get what we need."

"What's your story, anyway?"

"My story?"

"I know Hannah's a uni student. I know Haz works in video game development. But I don't know a thing about you."

Remy sighed. He didn't smile much. "I used to be into alternative medicinal treatment."

"You what?"

"Alternative medicine. Mindfulness training. Meditation. Presence. All kinds of teachings like that."

"Ah," I said.

"What's that supposed to mean?"

"Nothing. I just—"

"You think what I do is shit, don't you?"

"I didn't say that."

"You didn't have to. I see the looks on the faces of enough people as it is. But anyway. You don't have to worry about being indoctrinated by my clinic, or whatever. It got shut down just two days ago. Building repossessed. Honestly, I didn't have a whole lot left to fight for. And now... well, all I have left is myself. And you guys."

I felt better to finally have heard a bit of background from Remy. He was struggling, just like the rest of us. He was one of us.

"Let's make it quick," Hannah said when we got to the car park of the supermarket. In the distance, the buildings of Salford, all of them no doubt lacking power. "Haz. You know what we're looking for?"

"Of course," he said, sounding a lot more confident now.

"Good," Hannah said. "Then let's go in there."

Stepping inside the supermarket was like stepping into another world. It was weird. It was like we'd just been transported over to Universal Studios or somewhere like that, stepping into the middle of a dystopian movie set where people were terrified of something coming. People were scrambling down the aisles, stuffing their trolleys with way too much stuff. People were arguing over food, some of them getting physical. And all the time, the shop assistants weren't getting involved. They were gone, some of them. Others, well, they were fighting for what they wanted too.

I didn't honestly believe the world would lose its shit so soon into a blackout. But in a way, I'd been naive. Of course it was going to go this way. Every single electronic piece of equipment had fried. It wouldn't take long for people to realise they were going to have to fend for themselves until some kind of order returned.

"Is it worth even getting involved in this?" I asked.

"I have an idea," Hannah said.

She started to leave the supermarket.

"Hannah? Where are you—"

"Just follow me. I want to make this quick."

Even though I felt like time was running out, I followed Hannah outside, as did Haz and Remy.

"Okay," Haz said, as we walked through the car park. "I appreciate the need for fresh air, but I don't think we'll be finding much in the way of peanut butter and cheese out he... oh shit."

He'd stopped speaking because of what Hannah was doing.

She'd opened the back of a lorry. A delivery lorry.

And inside that lorry, undiscovered by the rest of the people... food. Water. Lots of it.

Looking over my shoulder, still unable to shake that fear that some security guard would be watching, I hesitantly climbed inside and started filling my rucksack with canned tuna, peanut butter, all kinds of quick and easy—but healthy and nutritious—snacks that would get me through for the time being. I didn't know how long "the time being" was going to consist of, so I had to be prepared.

"You want to make sure you've got some Super Noodles," Haz said. "We can boil water, and they'll really go far."

I put some into my rucksack, feeling much more positive, much more optimistic at our togetherness as a team.

I turned to Hannah, and I smiled. "Good job thinking of this. I wouldn't have thought of it in a million years."

She smiled back at me, eyes twinkling. "I know you wouldn't. So it's a good job I..."

She stopped.

All of us stopped.

We were just about ready to leave this lorry with everything we had when we saw someone standing right at the lorry door.

It was a family of four. A man. A woman. A little boy and a little girl.

Only the man was holding a knife.

"We need this stuff for our family. So you're gonna drop it and walk away from here. Now."

CHAPTER SIXTEEN

I looked at the man holding the knife, and I felt the most scared I'd felt since the power had gone out.

The sun glimmered down on him, reflecting against the blade of the knife. We were out of the sunlight, in here in the back of the truck, where we'd gathered our supplies. We hadn't expected anyone else to come join us in the middle of our search. We were foolish for being so naive, really. Of course someone was bound to come and join us. We weren't the only people who'd put two and two together, after all.

The scariest thing about the scene in front of us? It wasn't the knife. Not in isolation. After all, a knife in isolation was always going to be pretty scary.

But it was the fact that a man—ordinary looking, probably had a decent job—was standing in front of his two young children and threatening someone else with a knife, right in front of them.

They were the lengths he was willing to go to.

And this was only day one.

"We can talk this through," Hannah said, attempting to appeal to the man's better nature.

"No," the man said. "No, we can't. You're going to lower your bags, and you're going to get out of this truck."

"Or what?" Hannah said, tauntingly.

The man looked all of us in the eye. He didn't look totally certain about what he was doing. But I knew how he must feel as his family looked on in peril. He knew the severity of the situation. He'd seen it, just like we had. He was one of the lucky ones who was at least going to be partly prepared for the moment he realised the power wasn't coming back on at all.

But if he resembled the kind of people we all had to become, the kind of lengths we all had to go to, then I wasn't sure I was comfortable with any of this new reality at all.

"You need to think very carefully about what you're saying and doing here," Remy said, his voice calming. His hands were raised. I kind of hoped he would use some of his alternative medicine tricks on this man to get him to leave, but I knew I was clutching at straws. "There's four of us. And there's just one of you. We have the upper ground."

"And I have a knife."

"You've no idea what we have," Hannah cut in. I was surprised to hear her speak with so much conviction, but then that's the way we all had to act now, really, if we wanted to get through this situation. Haz included. *Me* included. "So be careful. Be very careful before you make your next step."

Silence followed. A tense, drawn-out silence. I saw the man looking at us with curiosity like he was starting to doubt his own convictions. Behind him, I saw his wife holding both of their children, who were crying.

And despite everything, I felt sympathy for the man and his family.

"This is how it's going to work," Remy said, taking a few steps towards the man. "You are going to lower the knife, and you're going to leave us alone."

The man lifted his knife higher and pushed it in Remy's direction. "No. No, that's not what's gonna happen."

"Relax, man. Please."

"Don't tell me to relax!"

I heard the tension splitting through the air, and I saw that this situation wasn't going to end well—for our people or his. In that flicker of a moment, I saw the options opening up before me: act fast. Act fast.

Before the man could say another word, I stepped forward.

"We aren't going to give up all our stuff," I said. "You have to see it from our perspective. We need to ride this blackout out just as much as you do."

"Then we don't have a deal—"

"Half our water," I said.

The man frowned. So too did Hannah.

"What?" the man said.

"There's four of us, and there's four of you. We split what we've found in here, in half. We let you walk away and forget this ever happened."

The man turned away slightly like he was trapped between a rock and a hard place over what to do next. "How do I know I can trust you?"

"You don't," I said. "But face it. You aren't going to get a better offer right now."

"Jason, why don't we just make our way to the bunker?"

"Ssh," the man—Jason—said. Then he looked back at me and the rest of our people. "You throw your stuff towards us. That way, we don't have to make contact."

I heard him, and I saw sense in what he was saying. There was a fear, of course, that he was just going to slam the doors of this lorry shut and leave us trapped in here.

But there was something else on my mind, now.

Something that Jason's wife had said.

"Okay," I said, lowering my rucksack. "I'm going to roll this over in your direction."

"Scott," Hannah said, fear on her face. "Are you sure? We don't have lots of stuff as it is."

I shrugged, defeated. "I don't see another option right now."

We rolled the water, the cans, and another load of what we had in the direction of Jason and his family. Jason stuck it all into a bag for life, which was snapping at the corners, something else that made me incredibly pitiful towards him. When he'd done, he stepped back and looked me in the eye.

"Thank you," he said, knife still in hand. But it looked so alien there, now. So out of place. "Really. We..."

He stopped speaking, then.

He looked around.

So too did his wife.

Her eyes widened.

"What is it?" Haz asked.

I moved to the edge of the lorry, and my stomach sank.

"We need to get away from here. Fast."

We gathered our stuff and, together with Jason and his family, after all, we ran.

A small group—a group we'd seen leading a scrap in the supermarket just minutes earlier—were running in our direction.

But at least, as we ran now, we *had* a direction.

The bunker that Jason's wife mentioned.

That was where we needed to find out about.

That was where we needed to go.

CHAPTER SEVENTEEN

Garry Carpenter had been counting down the days to his release, even though deep down, in his heart of hearts, he suspected he was never going to set foot outside prison ever again.

He didn't think much of it when the lights first went out.

Not at first.

It was a normal morning at HMP Prison Buckley Hall. Normal being another day of the same white-washed walls, Calvin snoring away and grinding his teeth on the bunk above him. Sometimes, he wanted just to reach up there and wrap his hands around Calvin's throat. At least he'd be saving him another trip to the dentist. As well as that, he'd be putting them both out of their misery. Calvin was always complaining and moaning about how much he missed his wife and kids. He'd been doing so ever since they'd been put in a cell together three years ago.

Of course, Garry had been in here far longer than Calvin. He'd spent the majority of his life inside.

But hey. It wasn't so bad. Not when you were at the top of the food chain.

The sun peeked in through the tiny windows. To Garry, everything was normal. He would leave his cell at his usual time for breakfast. Then, he'd go down to the mechanics to do some work. He was retraining as a car mechanic, a usable skill for when he got out. That was the fallibility of prisons. They pretended they were gearing you up for a great life on the outside, when in fact, he knew the truth. Everyone knew the truth.

The second they got out of this place, they were right at the bottom of the pack. The chances of becoming homeless, or re-offending, were far, far greater than the chances of walking into another job.

And that's part of why Garry didn't mind it inside.

He leaned over, his bed creaking underneath him, the springs poking through the mattress. Of course, being inside had its downsides. The beds were crap. The fact that he didn't have a woman to wake up beside, even crapper.

But at least he *had* a bed. There were times in his life on the outside that he didn't have a bed at all.

Steady progress.

He wasn't aware of it yet, but something had changed in Buckley Hall. A massive, drastic change that would turn everything on its head.

But a few of the other prisoners had realised it. And that was the first indication Garry got that something was wrong.

He heard a few mumbles of confrontation, of fighting, but he didn't do anything about it, not at first. He often heard fighting and confrontation these days, especially in the overcrowded states of the prisons.

He lost himself in the fantasy of what an *ideal* life on the outside would be like. No worries, no concerns. Money already in the bank. He could get a little flat, enjoy a quiet life.

Oh.

And most importantly, he'd get revenge on Clarissa for what she'd done to him.

For taking his children away.

Garry felt tension in his chest when he thought of Clarissa and his two children. He didn't mope about them like Calvin did. Instead, he just felt mad. So mad. He felt eager, determined, to act. He knew it would get him in trouble. He knew if he exacted the revenge he wanted to achieve, then he would be back in here for the rest of his life.

But that was a failed fantasy anyway because he wasn't getting out of this place.

He was already in here for his last revenge mission. And that mission cost four people their lives.

One, an accident, admittedly.

The other... yeah, maybe a police officer. Didn't exactly make his case clear cut.

But he'd done what he had to do to extinguish his demons and make himself feel better.

And he'd do it again in a heartbeat.

"Shit," he heard a voice mutter somewhere outside his cell. "The doors. They're... they're open."

He heard the voice, and it didn't shock him, not initially. Sometimes they let the prisoners out in batches, especially now the crowding problem had got serious.

But this sounded different.

"Get back in your cell, Stan."

"Security! We've got a problem in here. Security? Do you copy? Do you copy?"

He opened his eyes then and jolted upright.

He smelled blood. Not literally, of course. But he could tell from the rising tension that something was going down out there and that this was an opportunity he wasn't going to miss.

If doors were open, then he was going to find his way out.

He was going to take that one opportunity to get his revenge on Clarissa.

And nobody was going to stop him.

"Wake up," he said, banging on the foot of Calvin's bed. "Sounds like something's going on out there."

He walked over to the door, still not quite accepting, still in disbelief.

Then he pushed against the door.

The door opened up.

He looked outside, and he saw the chaos unfolding already. He saw guards scrapping with prisoners. He saw people crowding around the exit door, which the prisoners were desperately trying to guard, backing away slowly but surely like they were giving in.

"Security!" One of the guards shouted. "Security!"

Then, his voice was drowned out by shouting.

Garry cracked his knuckles and walked towards the door. He saw one of the prison officers, John, glaring at him—only not assertively anymore, but with fear.

"What?" Garry said, tensing his fists. "Got a problem?"

John stood there for a few seconds, walkie-talkie in hand.

Then he dropped it and ran away.

Garry took a deep breath and smiled. He walked through the prison, past the fighting prisoners, past the security guards trying to hold everything together.

He walked through the door. Down the corridor. Around the police, who were struggling to cope with the surge of people leaving the prison.

And then, he walked towards the main entrance, and he stepped outside.

He took a deep breath, then. In the distance, he saw a plane falling from the sky like all the damned power in the world had just gone away. Beside him, he heard the chatter of more prisoners, all of them in disbelief, all of them in awe.

"This place is ours now," one of them muttered, laughing with joy.

"No," Garry said. "This place isn't ours. This *world* is ours now."

CHAPTER EIGHTEEN

It was when the sun started to set that the real tension kicked in.

It was getting darker. Only very gradually, but it was noticeable. And as the sun set even further, I felt sick, right to my stomach. Even though I'd faced up to the fact that the power probably wasn't going to come back on anytime soon, I suppose I'd still held out hope that maybe I was wrong. That maybe, just maybe, this all was some kind of big mistake by the power companies and that a solution was being worked on right away.

Even with all the things I'd witnessed, I still chose to believe.

Even with all the things I'd seen, I believed.

Hospitals overspilling with sick patients desperate for care.

Helicopters crashing from the sky.

Tunnels backlogged with cars, all smashed against each other, the people inside left in the most awful conditions.

People scrambling for supplies, reverting to their most primal selves.

Perhaps it was just a case of me *wanting* to believe that the power was going to come back on. But as we headed towards a military bunker which Jason and his wife Sue—as well as his two kids, Holly and Aiden—were heading to, we knew we were in this for the night at least.

"So this bunker," I said, as we waded through a farmer's field. Cows looked on from a distance, clearly oblivious to everything that was going on, perhaps even granted an extra lease of life for a few days because of what was unfolding. We were doing our best to stay off the roads now. Avoiding people wasn't going to be possible forever, especially in an area of such urban surroundings, but we had to do our best to keep a low profile, while not moving too far from the cities and the towns, where we were relying on to get our supplies. "How do you know about it?"

Jason sighed. He'd mellowed a lot since he'd joined our group. "We used to live over that way," he said. "Used to joke that when the world went to shit, at least we had a nuclear fallout bunker in the back yard to hole up in. Just a pity we moved."

"And you're sure it's going to be... well, fit for purpose?"

Jason shrugged. "All I know is that it was still an active military site. Owned by the MOD. I think they use it for surveillance, something like that."

"Handy," Hannah said.

"We don't know for certain what kind of state it's going to be in," Sue said. "We don't know who's going to be in charge there. We don't really know anything. Just that... well, if it's a military presence, then there's a chance that people might be there, and those people might know what's going on."

"And if they don't?" Remy said.

Jason looked at his two kids, who were being remarkably well behaved considering the circumstances, treating this whole thing like it was just some big adventure. "Then I guess we cross that bridge when we come to it."

As we walked some more, it began to grow difficult. I'd had too much water; I knew that. I had to conserve. But building a conservation mindset wasn't easy when you didn't know how long you were conserving for.

I could feel sores on the bottom of my feet, and I knew that wasn't a good thing either. I'd have to find some better trainers when I had a chance.

I looked at everyone. Remy was speaking with Hannah. Jason and his family were staying close. Haz was on his own. He didn't look too comfortable.

"You okay?" I asked.

He looked at me like I'd taken him by surprise. "Me? Oh. Yeah, Scotty-boy. Yeah, I'm fine."

"You don't seem it," I said, walking alongside him.

"Just a long day. Pretty tired, that's all."

"What do you make of the new people?"

"Jason and Sue? They seem... okay. They're struggling, just like the rest of us. The kids are sweet, I guess."

"I hate kids."

"Yeah. Me too."

I smiled, and I caught Haz smiling too.

Just the elephant in the room to address now.

"What happened. Back at the tunnel..."

"Oh, that," Haz said, scratching the back of his neck. "I dunno what happened. I've never—I've never had that before."

"You suffer from anxiety, don't you?"

Haz looked at me like he was defeated—like I'd broken his facade right down. "Not... well, just a little. But not *bad* anxiety."

"I've seen 'not bad' anxiety before. I've had it myself. What happened to you in the tunnel... that was pretty bad."

"And you think you're making me feel better about things by grilling me for it?"

"That wasn't my intention."

"Maybe you should look at your own problems before digging into other people's."

"Hey," I said, raising my hands. "I'm just trying to help."

Haz eased off then. "I'm sorry. I just... sometimes I get mad when people question me like that. Reminds me too much of the..."

He stopped, then. I could sense that he'd slipped up. He hadn't meant to bring up whatever he'd just brought up. I could see from the look in his eyes he knew he'd messed up.

I didn't push him, though, as we continued our walk to the bunker. "I just want you to know you can talk. If ever you n—"

"I'm not a video games developer," Haz said.

"What?"

"When I told you I was a games developer. I'm not. I'm a twenty-eight-year-old dude bumming around in his mum's attic room claiming all the benefits I can because the crippling anxiety I've been dealt with won't let me go out into the world and actually find a job I desperately want."

I could see the colour return to Haz's cheeks when he spoke those words. It was as if he'd had something suffocating him for so long, and now the truth was out, he was so, so relieved.

"Don't tell anyone that," he said. "If you don't mind."

I put a hand on his back. "Course I don't. You just stay strong. And know that right now, we're all going through hell. Okay?"

He smiled. "Cheers, Scotty—"

"That still doesn't mean you can call me Scotty-boy."

The pair of us laughed as we joined up with the rest of the group, eager to reach the bunker before nightfall—eager not to be homeless for the first time in my life.

We knew we'd have to rest at some stage.

We knew we'd have to sleep.

But for now, we walked on, all eight of us, together.

We didn't think much of the sign for HMP Prison Buckley Hall when we walked past it.

CHAPTER NINETEEN

It soon became clear that we weren't going to find this bunker before nightfall.

We had been walking for a good few hours. The sky had gone orange, the threatening glow of darkness taunting us. The walking was becoming increasingly difficult. My feet were blistered to shit. Remy's weren't much better, neither were Haz's. It just seemed to be Hannah, Jason, Sue, and their kids storming onwards, all of them still determined that they could find what they'd set out to find before the darkness surrounded them.

Even more disconcerting was the fact that we were back in the suburbs. There were candles glowing in the windows of semi-detached houses, people standing at the end of driveways, looking at us through narrowed eyes as we passed. There seemed to be a pause on the conflict of the inner-cities here in the outskirts. The suburbs hadn't quite descended into the all-out chaos of the cities. There were a few crashed cars, here and there, and people sounded disgruntled.

But there was still order, here. I guessed that was because smaller communities like this had each other. They knew how to band together in times of crisis.

If only they knew that this wasn't just some normal power outage.

"It's about time we found somewhere to rest," I said.

The rest of the group slowed down, except for Jason. He kept on marching onwards, dragging his children along in the process. They had recently started crying, a sound that, while annoying, I had to sympathise with because they were clearly exhausted.

"Jason," Sue said.

Jason groaned. "Sue, we can't just slow down. You know as well as I do how important it is to get where we need to go—fast."

"Daddy, I'm tired," Holly said.

"Don't you worry, Hol," Jason said, putting a hand on his daughter's back. "We're going to be there in no time."

Jason kept on walking. It fast became clear that he didn't have any intentions of stopping at all. I didn't want to fall into some kind of conflict with him. But I didn't want to lose him, either. He was one of our group now.

"Jason," I said, stepping forward.

He spun around and squared right up to me. "What, Scott? Do you think you can do a better job of being a dad than I can? Do you think you know everything there is to know about parenting?"

"Please. We're just talking about taking a break."

"Yeah, well that's easy for you to say when you don't have any kids of your own, isn't it?"

I snapped, then. I couldn't control it, couldn't prevent it. I didn't often see red in my life, but this was one moment where the red took over, and I couldn't control myself.

I smacked my fist around Jason's face.

He didn't push back. My knuckles didn't bounce off him like maybe I'd expected.

Instead, he went falling right down to the ground in a heap.

"Scott!" Hannah called.

But I couldn't stop myself now. I couldn't stop myself now

that Jason was on the ground, while he was looking up at me, blood pooling from his left eye.

That smug face, and the thing he'd said. The horrible thing he'd said.

I saw flashes of Harriet's face, two weeks before her death.

I felt the fear I'd felt then. But also the excitement. The excitement, as we'd prepared to take another step in our lives. The biggest step of all.

I swung at Jason again, and I heard Sue screaming as more blood came from his head. Aiden and Holly were both crying now. Someone was pulling me, trying to drag me away, but still I just kept on trying to punch.

It wasn't the hatred towards Jason I felt.

It was hatred of the situation.

Hatred that I'd bottled up all this time since Harriet's death.

And as that pain filled my body, I couldn't swing another punch.

I could only let Remy and Hannah drag me away from Jason as I started crying.

"Don't you dare talk about me being a dad," I said, shaking my head, my entire body shivering with a whole cocktail of emotions.

Jason sat upright. He wiped at his bloodstained face. "You're mad. I won't have you anywhere near my family. Not anymore."

"Don't lecture me about being a dad!" I shouted.

I felt myself being dragged away, then. And then I knew there was more conflict, more words exchanged. But after that moment, it was mostly just a blur.

All I could think about was the happiness I'd felt when Harriet came home and told me what she'd found out.

And the pain I'd felt when I'd lost not one person that awful day, but two.

Four hours later, and we were sleeping in a tent in the garden of one of the suburban residents.

I was outside though. Jason and his family were in the tent, and he'd made it pretty clear that he didn't want me near him, or them. Sue told me he'd come around, in time, and to sneak in the tent when he was asleep, which never took him long. He'd acted stupidly himself and should've seen what happened coming.

But to be honest, I was still just trying to interpret what'd happened myself.

The way I'd flipped.

The way my emotions had spilled out in a way like they never had before.

"What happened back there," Hannah said, breaking the silence as I stared up at the stars. "You lost someone else. Didn't you?"

My chest tightened. Beside me, there was a cooking stove that Haz had set up to make us all some food that night. It had a simple push-button igniter and a two-litre pot. Really handy, for as long as we managed to keep hold of it. It'd save us having to start fires of our own, anyway, something which I was woefully clueless about.

As for what Hannah asked me... I didn't want to say the words. Because saying them crystallised a misery I hadn't even accepted yet. I'd only just about processed the deaths of my mother, of Harriet. The other death... I'd kept that one hidden away, bottled up, only now, it felt like the grief was spilling out.

Hannah put a hand on my shoulder. "You don't have to talk. No one's expecting you to. But you need to know that what happened back there... it can't happen again. Because if it happens again, then how are we any different to anyone else?"

I nodded. Part of me wanted to open up about my loss. How my daughter had died before I'd even known her, inside of Harriet's body that day she'd timed crossing the road just a little too late.

But I couldn't. I still couldn't.

I just had to appreciate that someone had finally, finally made me feel like it was okay to open up about it.

"I'm going to straighten things out with Jason tomorrow," I said, taking a deep breath and looking up at the stars again. "And then we're going to head to the bunker. All of us."

Hannah smiled. She kept her hand on my shoulder for a little while longer. Part of me wanted to tell her to keep it there. Part of me knew she wanted that, too.

But eventually, she disappeared inside the tent, leaving me alone on the outside.

"Goodnight," she said.

"Night."

She disappeared into the tent, and I sat alone, staring up at the stars.

I wanted to find this bunker.

I wanted to put things right.

But at the same time, I couldn't help being afraid.

Not just of the world on the outside. But of the whole world of pain inside me, too, just waiting to burst out some more…

CHAPTER TWENTY

I woke suddenly, freezing, to the sight of Jason standing over me.

I gasped as I shot upright. The sun shone down on me brightly, but I felt sick and shivery. It felt, partly, like I'd just woken up from a long, drawn-out nightmare, and I wanted to believe that that's all it was—a nightmare. All this rubbish about the power going down, about the world's electricity supplies collapsing, that was just a figment of my over-active imagination.

But then I felt the dew seeping through my trousers as I sat there beside a tent in the back of a garden, and I knew that it wasn't a nightmare at all.

That very reality made me vomit, right away.

"Scott," Jason was saying, his voice piercing to my ears. "It's Hannah," he was saying, but I didn't hear the rest of what he said because I lurched forward to vomit once again.

When I stopped vomiting, my eyes burning with the sensation, I lifted my head and looked up at Jason. I saw that he had cuts under his eyes, and it took me a moment to register that *I* had done that to him. I'd flipped yesterday when he'd confronted me about my ability to be a father. I knew I was in the wrong. I knew I shouldn't have lost it like I did.

But still, what he'd said to me hurt.

"Hannah's gone, Scott," he was saying, his voice still distant and somewhat unreal sounding. "She's gone."

It clicked, then.

Hannah.

Hannah, who I'd been with since the train broke down.

Hannah who I'd known since the start of this whole mess.

"Gone?" I said.

"We woke this morning and found the zip of her tent open. Weren't you last to see her?"

I heard a slight accusatory tone to Jason's voice, and part of me wanted to grill him on it. The other part of me knew he was probably right to be accusatory. I was the last to see her. I should've gone back in the tent.

Instead, I'd fallen to sleep right beside the tent.

I stood up, my head thumping. I didn't remember waking up at all through the night, but I could tell I'd had a goddamned awful sleep. "Do you think someone's been in here?"

"Holly said she saw her just getting up and leaving."

"And what time was that?"

Jason turned to Holly, who looked up at me while standing by her mum, Sue's, side as if she'd done something wrong.

"Sorry," I said. "Stupid question." Then I crouched opposite her. "Was it dark when you heard Hannah leave?"

Holly looked up at her mum for reassurance, who nodded at her. Then, chewing on one of her fingers, she said, "No. It was light, I think."

"Well if it was light, she can't have gone too far, wherever she's gone."

I started to walk away, out of the garden of this house and towards the streets.

"Where are you going?" Jason asked.

I looked back and frowned. "Well, if she's gone, I'm going to go look for her."

"It could be dangerous out there."

"It's the same world it's always been," I said.

Jason shook his head. "You don't know that. Not today."

We looked at one another, and I knew Jason had a point. A night had passed. When people woke up and realised that the power still wasn't back—and that they *still* had no idea what was happening—frustrations would peak to a whole new level.

But still, the time for standing aside was gone. I had to go find Hannah.

"I won't be long," I said, although I didn't say it too confidently. Probably because I knew, deep down, that there was no telling just how long it would take me to find Hannah at all.

"I'm coming with you."

I looked back again. Jason was walking towards me.

"You don't have to."

"No," he said. "You're right. We need to find her."

He kissed his daughters, then held Sue tightly.

"I'll be back in no time," he said.

"Do you have to do this, Jason?" Sue asked.

Jason smiled. Nodded. "Yes. Yes, I do."

WE WALKED down the road together. It was a cul-de-sac, so, fortunately, there was only one way for us to go. And therefore by definition, only one way for Hannah to go too. But it made sense to search the remaining houses in the streets before we cast our search net even further.

We were mostly silent, as was the rest of the street. We saw movement behind the curtains. People standing by their living room windows, tucking into bowls of Weetabix, oblivious to the fact that they might have to save some. In one of the driveways, two muscular men were trying to jumpstart their car—to no luck, naturally.

"Scuse me?" I said, walking over.

The men glanced at me like I wasn't from around here.

"We're looking for a woman."

"Aren't we all, mate?" He grinned.

I ignored his quip. "Dark hair. Bright blue eyes. Fairly tall. Pale-ish skin. Have you seen her go by this morning?"

The two men thought about it for a few seconds. "Not sure I did, mate. Sorry."

I felt my stomach sink. "Thanks anyway."

Jason and I walked further. We didn't say anything to each other. It was still pretty awkward, in truth.

It was Jason who broke the silence. "I'm sorry," he said. "For what happened yesterday."

I waved him off. "It's water under the bridge."

"I shouldn't have questioned you like that. It was a dick move to make. Especially... especially having lost a kid myself."

"I'm sorry to hear that too."

"Like you say. It's in the past. But it never truly escapes you. Not really."

He looked at me and smiled, and I looked back at him, and I smiled.

He held out a hand. "Let's start afresh."

I put my hand in his and shook. "Like we've never met."

"Except for the cuts and bruises."

"Could just pretend we got them go-karting or something."

"Go-karting?"

I shrugged. "First thing that came to mind."

Jason laughed. "Funny thing you mention go-karting. First date Sue and I went on, believe it or..."

He kept on speaking, but his voice faded into the background.

It faded because I could see her in the living room of the house across the road.

"Hannah," I said.

Jason frowned. Then he turned to look where I was looking. When he saw her, his jaw dropped. "Shit."

She was in the lounge of a detached house across the road. It was hard to see clearly through the glass, but one thing was for sure.

There were three young lads standing around her, hoods pulled up over their heads.

One of them was holding a knife.

Part of me wanted to run. It wanted to get away and out of here.

But I felt my fist tightening and I knew that as much as it terrified me, I couldn't just back down and give in. Not while Hannah was in danger.

"What do we—" Jason started.

But it was too late.

I was already running across the street, towards the house.

I stopped at the door. Part of me wanted to take the old-fashioned, polite route of knocking. But time could be of the essence.

So instead I just opened that door and stormed inside.

The men swung around and looked at me, clearly surprised. There was a dull smell of cannabis in the air.

The guy with the knife, wearing a grey hoodie, looked at me through gaunt, darkened eyes.

"Who the hell are you?"

Fight or flight took hold. I should walk away and get out of here. This wasn't my scene.

"Hey," he said, poking a knife in my direction. "You gonna answer my question or what?"

I saw then that Hannah was crying. She'd partly undone the buttons on her collar. It made me feel sick, knowing what might have gone down here if I hadn't got here soon.

I gritted my teeth together, no longer feeling fear but instead, pure rage. "Doesn't matter who I am. You're going to put that knife down and let Hannah leave."

"Hannah?" the man said, smiling with yellowed teeth. "Oh, you know her, do you? All we wanted was to see Hannah do a little dance for us, mate. Make the most of the whole no-police shit on our day release. Can't say you don't want to see that yourself, eh?"

I stepped towards him. He pointed the knife right back at me.

I looked him in the eye. I'd never stood up to anyone in my life like this before. I felt all the pent up times I'd wanted to building up and overspilling, right at this moment.

"Put the knife down," I said. "Let her leave. Now."

The man smiled, and I smelled the sourness of his breath. "Sorry, mate. But that ain't gonna—"

What happened next happened all too quickly.

I pushed at the man.

I lost my balance in the process.

The man swung out.

I heard a gasp. No, two gasps. Gasps from the two other hooded men, who were clearly just tagging along with their leader.

I looked at saw the horror in Hannah's eyes, too. And for a second, I wondered if I'd been stabbed, and I just hadn't registered the pain yet.

And then I looked around, and I saw what they were all gasping at.

Jason was holding his neck.

Blood was spurting out of it.

His face was pale.

"Jas..." I started.

But it was already too late.

Jason fell to the floor.

The light in his eyes was already fading...

CHAPTER TWENTY-ONE

When I reached the driveway to the house we were staying in, holding Jason in my arms, I knew he was already gone.

Hannah and I didn't say anything. We just put him to rest outside the wall of the house. Right away, a few neighbours came running out, gasping, horrified by what they were witnessing—the first realisation that this world was well and truly losing not only the power but its morals.

"I'll—" Hannah said.

"No," I said. "No, I'll go."

I tried to smile at Hannah, who half-smiled back at me, staying by Jason's side.

Then, heart racing, I walked down the driveway, around the gate, into the garden.

Holly and Aiden were running in circles after one another. They were laughing and giggling. They looked so oblivious to all the horrors outside. So naive.

I wished I could let them stay like that forever.

Then, Sue stepped out of the tent.

When she saw me, her eyes widened. She smiled, clearly relieved to see me.

And then her face dropped. Her eyes narrowed.

"Jason?" she said. "Where's…"

"I'm sorry, Sue," I said, a frog bouncing around my throat, tears building in my eyes. I shook my head. "I'm so sorry."

I didn't have to say anything else.

Sue fell to her knees.

And in the gentle trickle of rain, she wailed.

CHAPTER TWENTY-TWO

I dug my spade into the solid earth deep enough to fit Jason's body into it.

The sun peeked through the clouds, but specks of rain fell. The wind was strong. Around us, there wasn't just Sue and her two children—there wasn't just Remy, Hannah and Haz, either. There wasn't even just the people in whose garden we were staying. There were a few people from the houses nearby, who had never known Jason, all of them walking by to pay their respects.

Sue was in bits. Her children wouldn't stop crying. I'd thought about just burying Jason's body, but Suli, who worked at a local funeral parlour, gave us a coffin. "Pay me back when we're back online," he said.

Even when he said it, I wasn't sure if he totally believed that there was going to be such a thing as "back online". But I appreciated the gesture.

When I'd dug the hole, I looked at Haz, who'd helped me dig it. He was sweating and panting, probably some of the most intensive exercise he'd ever done in his life these last couple of days.

I nodded at him as I crouched down to lift the coffin, and he nodded back at me.

We lowered it in, holding on to bands on each side so it didn't drop down. It was so heavy, though, and then it hit me in full force that I was lowering a human body into the earth. And yet in spite of what I was doing, after having witnessed first hand a death for the first time (I hadn't been there when they'd turned the life support off Harriet's machine), the world didn't feel any different. Life still went on. I still had the same aches and pains in my body, the same sickly tastes in my mouth.

Life hadn't gone on pause, either. We couldn't just step back and wait for the old world to come along again. That wasn't going to happen. Now, there was going to have to be an adaptation to a new way.

The coffin hit the ground below. And when it landed, I heard Sue let out an audible whimper, like she was finally facing up to a shocking reality that her husband wasn't with her anymore.

It was cruel. It was impossible. Yesterday, they were no doubt just sitting around with their children getting ready for another normal day.

The power had gone, and the world had changed.

I looked around and saw people were looking at me like they were expecting me to say something.

I felt my cheeks blushing. I wanted to step into the background. But I soon realised I couldn't just walk away from my responsibilities, not now.

"I didn't know Jason for long," I said, as the rain fell heavier. "And we... we didn't get off to the best start. But I know one thing. He was a good man. A good man who cared about his family very much. And more than anything, he'd have wanted us to make sure we get his family to that military bunker he told us about."

Remy nodded. Hannah sighed and smiled flatly out of obligation.

"So that's what we're going to do," I said. "We're going to make our way to that bunker, and we're going to honour Jason's memory."

I looked down at the hole in the ground.

But in my mind, I couldn't get something else out of my head.

What that man had said about "day release".

The people who'd taken Hannah and killed Jason were prisoners.

So prisoners were escaping. And they were making their mark on the world already.

"We're going to make it," I said. "For Jason."

Then I dug the earth back down and threw the soil onto Jason's coffin.

I wanted to avenge Jason's death.

I wanted to roll back time and make it so that I'd taken the blade instead of him.

I wanted to hold those who'd killed him—and been willing to do God-knows-what to Hannah, too—to justice.

But I couldn't.

All I could do was dig, as the rain fell heavier, and a bright rainbow arced across the sky, hopefully in promise of a better future...

"JESUS CHRIST, Garry. Why did you have to get all frigging happy with the knife back there?"

Garry sat just outside of the suburban town they'd been holed up in for the night with Mitch and Peter beside him. They were on a hill, looking down at the houses in the suburbs. It was nice to be getting some fresh air again, even if there was rain in the air now. The rain didn't bother him as much as it used to. Mostly he was just grateful to be on the outside again.

Besides. He'd done what he'd got out of prison to do.

Everything was sweet now.

"I mean, you coulda just told 'um to piss off," Mitch whined. "They'd have heard us loud enough. Now I'm gonna end up going back inside for the shit you've done."

Garry ignored Mitch. He wiped the bloodied knife against his leg. Unlike Mitch, Garry had figured out that they weren't going back to prison anytime soon, not if the rumours about the mass blackout and power outage was true. They could get far away, and there'd be no way of tracking them. Besides, if there really had been a power outage, then every single prison in the country was gonna be causing problems for the police as soon as the power came back on.

If the power came back on.

He'd just be one in a long line of inmates that the country would attempt to get back inside.

Good frigging luck with that.

"I mean, what now?" Mitch droned on. "We supposed to just walk around and wait for them to lock us up again? 'Cause I won't go down for murder, mate. I was two years off being released. I won't have fifteen years added to my—"

"Then walk," Garry said.

He looked at Mitch, and at Peter, and he saw the fear in both of their eyes. It was strange seeing them out of their prison gear and in normal hoodies. To be honest, he hadn't asked for anyone to come with him. They'd just gravitated towards him when he'd made his way into the suburbs, towards the nice little family home where his ex-wife was living...

He'd done what he had to do.

He'd made her pay for taking his children away from him.

And the hardest thing of all?

His kids had already moved out with some other man.

The bitch had let the kids go, after everything.

At least she wasn't a problem anymore.

Then there was the man he'd stabbed...

He had to admit he felt a bit shitty about that. After all, he wasn't the one standing up to him. He'd just got in the way.

They'd fled soon after. And something inside Garry let Hannah and her fella leave with Jason—as he was called—in their arms. He'd taken one of them, made them pay, and so he'd let them go, learning their lesson.

But as he watched them leave, he'd seen the man who'd stood up to him look him right in the eye with such a hate that he feared it would stay with him for a long time.

"So what *do* we do?" Mitch asked, not quite as whiny anymore.

Garry gritted his teeth together. He looked down at the house where his wife had lived, and at the small trail of blood that had fallen from Jason's neck as that duo had carried him down the street, in an attempt to save him.

"We see what we can get from this situation," Garry said, as a rainbow formed over the beautiful suburban land. "From this world."

CHAPTER TWENTY-THREE

Another day of walking and suddenly this new world started to feel like a very pertinent reality after all.

The sun was hidden behind the clouds, which were thickening by the hour. To be honest, I had a fear in the pit of my stomach, and that fear was night. We'd been allowed to take the tent that suburban family had let us stay in with us to the bunker, in case our journey took longer than a day. Admittedly, we'd had to trade a few things, but that was the way of the world now. Anyway, according to Jason's instructions, we weren't all that far off. Soon, we'd be back to something like normality.

But that was the problem. Jason was dead, now. We were relying on a mixture of Sue's faint—and grief-stricken—knowledge, road signs, and our own intuition. Neither were a great mix.

We'd been trying to stray off the beaten track for some time now, but we weren't having much luck. It was just suburb after suburb, each of them the same in their dim hopes that the power was going to return at some stage. Every supermarket we passed was a scene of chaos and panic, now. Honestly, I'd never believed the world would fall so quickly when shit went down, quite in the way it had. I'd always thought—and hoped—that people could pull their shit together in the face of a disaster.

I was fast realising that those hopes were misplaced. Of course people were going to lose their shit. Everything they'd worked for, everything they'd spent their money on, everything they'd *invested* in—and not just financially, but mentally, like the internet and the news and pornography—all of it was gone.

And I was just expecting them to pick up the pieces and band together like nothing had changed?

"I'm thinking we're almost at the stage where we're gonna have to eat rats," Haz said, mournfully.

"Don't be disgusting," Hannah said.

"What? I'm just being realistic. Our nicely packaged food isn't gonna last forever. We've got a decent portable stove. Besides, I don't think the peanut butter crackers are really doing it for me anymore."

"It'll do you good," Hannah said.

"What? Are you saying I'm—"

"Yeah," she said. "You're overweight. You know you are. Not point hiding from it."

I saw Haz's cheeks blush, a wave of shame covering him, much like the time he'd confided in me.

"So just don't worry. You aren't gonna die because you're suddenly only getting... shit. Less than a thousand calories if you include all the exercise, probably."

That thought made me feel tense. I wasn't the heaviest of guys. I lost weight easily. I knew it was going to take its toll on me, all this exercise combined with a lack of food.

Besides, what if I got sick? We'd have to think about hydration. Because like the food issues, water was going to be a problem too.

Unless we could think of a way to make water on the outside safe for drinking.

"Haz," I said, interrupting his and Hannah's bickering. "You said a day ago that you knew a thing or two about survival methods. Stuff like that."

He scratched his head and frowned. "Only what I've read on the internet and played in games."

"How about making water safe for drinking? Know anything like that?"

He looked like he was mulling it over for a few seconds. Then his eyes lit up. "I... I mean I don't know if it'll work, but—"

"But you're willing to try?"

Haz nodded. Right.

We found a large aluminium bottle inside one of our packs, which Haz had picked up to pool our water bottles together to save space.

"Now, the best place to get water is from somewhere without people, manmade things. Stuff like that. Streams, basically."

I looked around at our surroundings. We were still in suburbia. "Not sure we'll have much chance of that around here."

"It's fine," Haz said, shaking his head. "We can just boil the water ourselves. Besides, we can grab a few filters on the way. They should take the dirt and the bacteria out of it. Oh, and there's Tincture of Iodine, too. Two per cent, I think. They kill viruses and bacteria. Or even just a bit of bleach."

"Bleach?" Hannah gasped. "I'm not drinking bleach. Feel free to go ahead, though."

I knew we were still a way from needing to gather our own water. But it was handy to have someone with Haz's knowledge, however basic, around.

Tincture of Iodine. Boiling water. Or drinking from a water source that is way away from humans or machinery. All foolproof methods.

And if we got ill, well. There was always an abundance of hospitals to...

Oh, wait. No there wasn't. Not anymore.

"Honestly, though," Haz said, "there's a few other ways.

Layering a bottle with sediment and filters and pouring the water through it, but that's when we're *really* struggling. But to be honest, if we have to make a choice between chugging water that might be dirty and getting dehydrated, you've just gotta drink the water anyway. Bacteria might kill you. Dehydration definitely, definitely will."

Sue sniffed. She hadn't said a word since they'd set off besides the basic directions. But she opened her mouth and said, "We're going to be at the bunker soon. We won't have to worry about all this for long."

I wished I shared Sue's confidence.

We walked further. And as we walked, Remy up ahead, Hannah further back, Haz by my side, I spoke to him about all these contraptions and survival methods he knew. He told me about using batteries to start fires. You basically had to connect the positive and negative terminals with a wire or some foil to create a spark. It seemed so simple, something I imagined so many people knew about, and yet I was so naive about these things.

Similarly, he blew my mind about all other kinds of "prepping" tips he'd learned. Apparently, a good way to secure electronic devices before EMP events were Faraday Boxes. They are basically made from metal filing cabinets, biscuit tins, that kind of thing. However, the device you are trying to protect must be insulated and not touching the metal. If you wrapped a good spread of aluminium foil around the box, then theoretically, your device should survive.

Just a pity nobody really took prepping seriously in this country.

"All this knowledge," I said, "and you're worried you're never going to get a job."

Haz stopped, then. He frowned at me. "This knowledge? It's just silly stuff that's stuck in my head after reading too many dystopian novels and spending late nights on conspiracy websites. It's not exactly gonna get me a job."

I shrugged. "Maybe not in the old world. But in the new world…"

It felt weird to be saying those words just one day into a changed world. But this, for sure, was something that had meaning. Haz could use his skills, if the power returned, to make people aware of survival, and what to do in case of emergency. A business like that would boom.

And if the power didn't return…

Well. People like Haz were going to be in very strong demand.

"It's here," Sue said.

I barely registered what she'd said until I saw the tall, green structure right over a field in front of us. We were just outside the suburbs now, on a country lane.

"Is that…" I started.

"It's the bunker," Sue said, turning around and smiling for the first time since the death of her husband. "We made it."

CHAPTER TWENTY-FOUR

I saw the bunker in the distance, and for the first time in a long time, I felt hope.

The sun was setting, which really captured just how long we'd been walking. I was still in the habit of checking my wrist for the time, but of course, it was still jammed at that same time it had been at when the power had gone completely. Eight thirty-one. The time everything changed.

In a sense, though, I was growing less reliant on time, and that felt kind of liberating in spite of the initial difficulties adjusting to it. All that mattered, really, was the position of the sun in the sky. If the sun was lowering, then that meant darkness was coming, and we needed to find shelter.

Of course, we could keep moving in the dark and shelter in the day. That was a possibility we'd discussed; after all, the bulk of people in positions like us would be travelling in the day and resting at night. But we needed sleep, and I guess there was still a naivety deep within that didn't want to mess up our body clocks. We wanted to maintain some level of order, of normality. Suddenly shifting our body clock was too much of a change so early in the fall.

The fall. What a thing to call it. What a way to think of it.

And yet it struck up such images.

Society, falling.

Everything around, collapsing.

But this here—this bunker—this was going to change everything.

Sue led the way, eagerly, her children's hands in hers. It was like she was running back towards Jason, living naively under the impression that if she got there, she'd be reunited in some way. That she'd be able to bring him back from the dead.

Such was the shock of grief.

And the real grieving surely hadn't even hit yet. Not in earnest.

"Wait up," I said, jogging closer to Sue. Remy, Hannah, and Haz weren't far away. "We should take it easy when we're approaching. We don't know for certain everything's going to be in order here."

"Even if it's not," Sue said, "it's shelter. It's getting dark. Maybe... maybe we're the first ones here."

Part of me kind of wanted that to be the case. Not because I *wanted* to be left to fend for myself. But because I feared what kind of people might already be in this place.

I'd seen what the prisoners who'd attacked and killed Jason were capable of. Who was to say there weren't more people like them? Who was to say they couldn't just do it again?

As we ran, I caught Hannah smiling at me. I knew what that smile was. I knew what that look in her eyes was. It was hope.

"This could be it," she said as if the nightmare was on the verge of coming to a swift end. "This could really be it."

I let myself feel that hope for a second. And I knew I'd made a mistake right then because if anything went wrong, then the pain of the fall was going to be even worse.

I knew something was ahead when I saw movement.

I glanced up.

"Did you see that?" Remy asked. So not just me, then.

I squinted into the distance, past the solid green gates of the bunker grounds. They were high, but nothing we couldn't scale if we tried really hard.

I couldn't see any more movement.

"We keep going," I said. And as we got closer, I felt cautious, and I realised it was about time I and everyone else found some kind of weapon to use in case of another confrontation. Sure, we had a few sticks and things like that, and a multi-tool that Haz insisted was for survival more than confrontation. But we couldn't have another Jason incident. We couldn't let that happen. "But we keep it stead—"

"Mummy, did you see the army men?"

Holly's words went over my head at first. But then I saw them too, and I realised—with a surge of hope—that Holly was right.

Standing at the gates, right at the other side, there were four men. They were all geared up in camo gear from head to toe. They were armed.

"Shit," Hannah said. "This is it. They've—they're using this place. Some kind of temporary shelter."

But as we got closer, my hope started to shift into doubt. I saw that the soldiers didn't exactly look welcoming. They looked... disorganised. Like they weren't sure what to do.

And then they raised their guns.

We stopped, right there.

All of us stopped, except for Sue, Holly and Aiden's hands in hers.

"Sue!" Hannah called.

"Don't make another move," the soldier in the middle said. He had dark circles under his eyes. He didn't look like he'd had much sleep.

Sue still stumbled forwards, gripping tightly onto her children's hands. "Please," she said. "We've come so far. We just want—"

Then, something happened.

Something unexpected.

Something awful.

The soldiers fired.

The sound of gunfire was louder and more cracking than I'd ever expected. Being a Brit, I'd never heard any real gunfire, like the vast majority of Brits.

I couldn't get over how... well, intimidating it was. How *scary* it was.

When I'd got over the sound, which still rattled around my ears, I looked around desperately. Those soldiers. They'd fired.

Sue.

Sue and the kids.

Were they...

When I looked ahead, I saw that Sue was still standing.

Both her children were still standing.

Relief filled my body, and I fell to my knees.

But as I fell, that relief soon turned into dread when I realised that these soldiers weren't messing around. Not one bit.

"Don't make us fire again," the middle soldier said. "Next time, we can't promise we will miss. And we really, really don't want to have to shoot you."

"What the hell's going on here?" Remy shouted, raising his arms. "Why are you firing at us?"

The soldier in the middle looked at the one to his right, somewhat mournfully.

Then he looked back at us. "There's no room here to sustain any more people. Not for long."

"What?" Hannah called. "But that can't be possible. You're supposed to be the army. You're meant to have things in order."

The soldier in the middle shook his head again. "I'm sorry, Miss. But there is no order anymore."

When he said those words, it really hit me.

It really, really hit me.

The army didn't know what was going on.

Nobody—nobody even in authority—knew what was going to happen next.

It was everyone for themselves, now.

There was no hierarchy.

There was only chaos.

There was only survival.

CHAPTER TWENTY-FIVE

We sat outside the tent, under the stars, shivering.

It was dark out here in the middle of nowhere. Far darker than it had seemed in the suburban family garden last night. It was impossible to believe another day had passed by already. But one thing was for certain—the fact that so long had passed meant that things weren't straightening out anytime soon.

And that was something I had to look in the mirror and accept.

Haz was struggling to start a fire. He insisted he knew how to start one manually—the battery method, the matchstick method; even a method called the hand drill, which needed nothing more than some wood, hands, and a hell of a lot of perseverance—but as it stood, he was having problems even getting one going with a lighter. The wind was strong, and it rippled against the walls of the tent, and specks of rain fell and dampened the wood.

And all this time, I couldn't do anything but sit in silence.

I couldn't help staring at the road ahead, realising I needed to make a choice.

The bunker had been a dead end. In the end, more powerful

people than my group had got there and taken it as their own. Whether that was right or wrong, it didn't really matter. What mattered was they had guns. They had weapons. Therefore, they had power.

It was a bitter pill to swallow, knowing we had just been outright rejected entry into what could be a safe place. But I'd heard what the soldier said. The bunker was only large enough to sustain a certain amount of people. Which meant that its resources weren't infinite. They were going to run out, eventually.

And when they did... who would stand a better chance of surviving once they got out into the outside world?

Those people in the bunker, who had been used to having everything delivered on a plate to them?

Or me and my people, after we'd spent time in this world, learning, adapting, surviving?

I turned around, then. I stood up, over Haz, Hannah, Remy, Sue and her two children, Holly and Aiden.

They all looked up at me like I was mad.

"I know this is tough to take. I know it's not what you want to hear. But we need to stop reacting to this situation now. We need to stop searching, wandering. We need to start fighting. For ourselves. Because if we don't, then this world isn't going to show any mercy."

Sue shook her head. "I'm not strong enough to survive. Not on my own."

"You are strong enough," I said. "And you aren't on your own. None of us are. We have each other."

Hannah puffed out her lips. "All fair and well making a grand pitch at surviving. But what the hell do I know about survival? What does either of us know about survival? What does *any* of us know about survival, really? Sorry, Haz."

Haz barely budged. He was used to Hannah shooting him down by now.

"We might not know things," I said. "But what do you do when you haven't revised for an exam?"

"You spend the night before cramming?" Haz said.

"No. You wing it. You use your intuition. You base your answers on what you do know."

"So," Sue said, snivelling. "What you're saying is... your grand plan is that we should *guess* our way to survival?"

"Not so much guess," I said. "Call it what you want. We might not know a lot about how to survive. But if we want to survive, we're going to have to find a way."

I saw their faces turning, then. Like a light was sparking in each and every one of them. Like they were coming around to what I was saying. "How can you be so... cool, about this?"

I was surprised to hear Sue say that. I was anything but cool. "I guess with what I've gone through this last year, I just... I've found a way to get through things. Even when I don't think I can. I don't know if I believe in a God, but I do believe that things tend to work out if I'm willing to fight for them. 'We rejoice in our sufferings, knowing that suffering produces endurance, and endurance produces character, and character produces hope.'"

Sue smiled. "Romans 5:3-4. That was one of Jason's favourites."

I smiled back at her, felt our collective loss.

"So what do you say?" I said, attempting to sound more hopeful now. "We might not be experts, but we know we need four things. Shelter. Water. Fire. Food. So we can work on getting better at those four things. Can't we?"

I saw a few muted nods.

"Can't we?" I repeated.

"Yes," everyone said, a lot more enthusiastically now.

I smiled, feeling like a leader for the first time in a long time. I was scared. Of course I was scared.

But I just had to swallow that fear and put it to the back of my mind.

I had to live in a day-tight compartment and take things one step at a time.

"Good," I said. "Now, we sleep. Then tomorrow, we begin."

"Begin what, exactly?" Sue asked, still sounding sceptical.

I looked up at the stars shining down brightly from above. "Surviving."

CHAPTER TWENTY-SIX

It was some time mid-afternoon the following day, and we were finally trying our luck at catching our own food.

Of course, we could take the easy route. We could work our ways into the towns and salvage the shelves for supplies. We were only just outside the suburbs, and those suburbs were only just outside the nearby town of Bolton, so it wasn't like the option wasn't there or anything.

But the truth was, we knew we had to get stronger. All of us. We knew that if the world was going to be the way it was currently—powerless—for a while, that we needed to build our skill set. After all, building that skill set would put us at an advantage over the rest of the population, as well as giving ourselves a higher value somewhere down the line. Maybe we would find our way to a community when communities began to forge. If we had skills—evidence that we were well adapted to this world—then we would be valued higher than the average person.

And what better way to build our skill set than start by hunting?

"I'm really not sure how I feel about this," Sue said.

She was struggling still. Of course she was. She'd just lost her husband, and things hadn't stopped moving since then. But she was doing remarkably well for a woman who'd just lost their love. She was holding things together, for the sake of her kids.

I put a hand on her back. "Hey. None of us are comfortable with this. Not really. But if the power isn't going to come back—"

"We need skills. I know. It's just… I guess I think about my children. What this might do to them."

"Think about what might happen to them if they *don't* know these things."

Sue tilted her head like she was considering the awful possibility that her children might end up all alone in this world someday. "And if the power comes back on?"

"Then that's a good thing, isn't it?"

"You've seen the chaos. You've seen the mess. You can't possibly just believe everyone will revert to normal when they realise just how easily things can be toppled."

I agreed with Sue. I couldn't see the world just clicking back to normality. Too many people had lost, and so many things had happened in such a short space of time for that to be the case.

Thankfully, Haz broke the silence before I had a chance to answer. "Right. I think I've done it. Think it's in place."

I walked over to Haz's side and looked at the trap he'd made. It was a ground snare, designed to catch smaller animals like squirrels, rabbits, that kind of thing. There was a piece of wire wrapped around a tree branch, then tied in a noose. In the ground, there were three smaller twigs with forked ends holding that noose up at head height. The idea was that a small animal would run through it and be captured.

I winced a little at the thought of what Harriet and her veggie ways would think of me involving myself in something like this.

"And you're sure this will work?" I asked

Haz shrugged. "It worked on video games. And I read somewhere that it's a pretty good trapping method. Just got to be patient, you know?"

"And if it doesn't?" Hannah said, walking over to the side of the trap. She looked down at it like it wasn't much cop, but like all of us, she was surely hoping that it would work.

Haz shrugged. "Then I'm sure I'll be able to scour the archives of my mind for another method. There's one called a spring deadfall. You bait a rock propped up by a stick and then—"

"Okay," I said, feeling queasy. "We get the picture. Just... let's see if this works out first."

We waited for a long time, right by the side of the tent. We lay stomach flat in the grass, watching the trap, just waiting for something to happen.

"What kind of animal are we supposed to be waiting for?" I whispered to Haz.

"Any will do. But this trap should be suited more for a rabbit or squirrel than anything too big."

"Hmm," I said.

"What?"

"Nothing."

"You don't think it'll work, do you?"

"It's not that I don't think it'll work."

"That's what people usually say when they don't think something will work."

"Look. I'm just holding out hope, that's all."

I wasn't sure how much longer we waited in silence. I looked around, saw that Sue and her kids were further back. Her kids were clearly growing bored. Sue just looked pale and jaded. *Stay in there, Sue.*

I looked at Hannah then, and I smiled. She smiled back at me. It was a while since we'd had a proper conversation. Thinking about it, I didn't really know much about Hannah's life, aside from the fact she'd been a mature student at Manchester Met University. She kept things awfully guarded. There just never seemed to be a right time or place to speak.

Then there was Remy. He was as quiet as ever. Clearly, he was a decent guy. A peaceful guy. And he looked like he wasn't sure about catching an animal himself.

We decided to pull back after what felt like hours to the tent, so we could check on the trap later. In that time, Haz spoke about other methods he knew of and an action plan of how we could create some kind of secure base. There were options, outside of living in a tent forever. Prisons, which would now be mostly emptied, but an idea which was a bit too *The Walking Dead* for my liking. There was talk of more bunkers or plans to get to the coast to see if any kind of emergency evacuation could be set up—even if it did seem all engines were fried. We even discussed getting a paddleboat of our own and attempting to make our way across the sea. It would be dangerous. Treacherous, even. But at least that way we could see just how widespread this darkness was.

It was a little while later that we heard a snap.

I looked at Haz. His eyes widened, and he looked back at me. Just in time. I was growing extremely hungry and couldn't stomach the thought of another slab of peanut butter and cheese.

Both of us ran out of the tent, battling to be at the front of one another.

"First dibs on the legs," Haz said.

"Oh, you can have them," I said. "I'll take the loin if I can..."

We stopped, then.

Total horror filled my body.

Right in front of us, there was something caught in the trap.

But it wasn't a rabbit.

It wasn't even a deer.

It was a dog. Its paw was stuck in the noose. The noose was wrapped around it. Tightly.

"Shit," I said.

The dog was a German Shepherd. It was whining badly. I could see its paw was bleeding with the tightness of the noose, and its eye-whites were on show.

"Didn't you plan for shit like this?" I said, angrily, as I approached the dog.

"How was I supposed to know?"

"Just shut up a minute." I got closer to the dog. "Hey, boy. If you are a boy. I'm just going on... Oh, yeah. Yeah, you are a boy. What're you called? Obviously, I've no idea what you're called, and neither have you, and here I am speaking to a dog like you're a human. Totally normal."

I got closer, feeling gradually nervous. I'd never really been a dog person. Not that I didn't *like* them—I just struggled to communicate with them.

But as I got closer to this dog, I felt a right to free it, and let it go.

Even if I was worried it might snap my fingers off.

The dog whined as I got closer, looking nervously between Haz and me.

"Ssh," I said. "It's okay. I've got you. You just... you keep still. Good boy. Good boy."

He wagged his tail a little when I said that.

And right then, I reached out and yanked the trap away from his paw.

He yelped. And for a split second, I didn't realise what'd happened until I saw the blood and felt a searing pain down my hand, then realised that the dog had bitten me.

"Damn it," I said, falling back, as the dog backed away, limping on its paw. "It bit me!"

"Ssh."

"What do you mean, ssh? He bit me. He—"

Haz covered my mouth then.

It took me a moment to realise why.

There was a noise.

But it was a noise that I hadn't heard for quite some time.

"Does it mean..." Haz started.

"I don't know," I said, as I watched the dog disappear into the trees. He turned around, looked at me, then limped away. "I don't know."

There was no mistaking the noise, though.

The sound of a car engine, revving up.

The sound of *power*.

CHAPTER TWENTY-SEVEN

I heard the revving of the engine once again, and this time, there was no denying what I was hearing.

I stood in the middle of the woods. My hand was still stinging, bleeding from where the dog I'd saved from our trap had bitten it. But that pain seeped into the background, now. It seemed irrelevant. *Everything* seemed irrelevant, all because of that engine sound.

Hannah crunched across the twigs. "What're you guys—"

"Ssh!" I said.

She frowned, then looked at my hand. "Scott. You're bleeding. You realise that, right?"

"Quiet," I said, blood trickling down my hand. "Listen."

She stopped. And soon, Haz, Remy, Sue and the kids were by our side.

All of them were listening to the sound.

All of them knew what it was.

"Does this mean the power's back?" Hannah asked.

Remy pulled his phone out of his pocket. He tried to switch it back on. "Doesn't seem to be the case."

"Then how is this happening?" Sue asked.

I wanted to give an answer. I wanted to help put their thoughts and suspicions at ease. But what could I say? After all, just like them, I didn't understand what was happening here.

I just knew that something was different.

Something was wrong.

"We have to check it out," I said.

Sue shook her head. "It's too dangerous."

"Too dangerous?" I said. "That you hear is power. And we've seen for ourselves that all power has been fried. You seriously suggesting we just back off and leave this?"

I saw the frown lines on Sue's face, and I felt a twinge of guilt for confronting her so hard, especially so soon after the death of her husband. "I just—my children."

"You don't have to come. You can stay back if you want to. But I'm going. And whoever wants to come with me... you're welcome. Okay?"

Remy stepped forward. "Don't see any other way forward."

Hannah shrugged, stepped to my side. "Me neither. Haz?"

Haz's cheeks flushed. Sweat was visible on his forehead. "Ah, shit. I shoulda known sticking around with you guys was a bad idea."

He walked ahead and joined us, leaving just Sue and her kids on their own.

"Sue," I said, looking back at her. I didn't want to leave her alone, but at the same time, I wasn't going to let her hold us back, either.

She shook her head. "I can't put my children in danger."

"We've got your back. We've got each other's backs."

"I trust you. I do. It's just..."

"I see it," Remy said.

I didn't know what he was talking about at first. Not until I turned around and headed to his side.

When I got to his side, I peeked through the trees to see what he was talking about.

And right then, I saw it too.

There was a house. A cottage, right in the thick of the woods. It was one of those old grey-bricked buildings, a run-down farmhouse type, with a large metal garage.

Inside the garage, there was a car.

It was an old looking car. Bit of a rust bucket.

But, petrol canisters by its side, its engine was running.

"So we see for definite now the car's running," Hannah said.

I realised then that Sue and her kids were by my side. They'd joined us, without announcing as much. At least I could feel good about that.

"What do we do?" Haz asked. "I mean, we can't just go over there. We can't just take it. Right?"

"It's a car," Hannah said. "It's there for the taking. We need to make the most of this. We might not get another chance."

"I'm not sure," Sue said. "I mean, it could be some kind of setup. Some kind of trap."

"Perhaps if we just approach them," I said.

"And say what?" Hannah said. "Hey, we like the look of your car; can we borrow it for a while?"

"Not exactly like that."

"No. Not like that at all. We take this car. Whoever owns it, they'd do the same to us."

A bitter taste filled my mouth. I felt twin hands tugging from either direction. My old self was telling me to be peaceful about this. To either approach the cottage amicably or to move on altogether.

But another voice—a newer voice inside my head—was telling me something very different.

It was telling me to go over there and take it because that was the kind of thing that kept me alive.

"Scott?" Remy said. "Any ideas?"

I swallowed a lump in my throat. I looked from Remy to

Hannah to Haz and to Sue and their kids. "We at least need to go over there. To see what we're dealing with."

"I have a bad feeling about this," Sue said. "A really bad feeling."

We moved on regardless. As we stepped out of the trees and into the garden of this house, getting closer to the rumbling engine, I felt exposed. I'd seen what people were capable of already. Hell knows what they'd do if they came across a group trying to steal from them.

I knew I wasn't even sure how far I'd be able to go myself if someone did the same to me.

And this was still the first week.

We walked slower through the grass. And as we got closer, I realised that the car door was open, and nobody was around.

We could just climb in there and take it. Drive our way down the gap between the trees. We could use the car as shelter. Find places off the beaten track to stay in. Travel the country in search of a real shelter.

I was beginning to salivate at the thought.

"Scott," Remy said. "You see this?"

I looked to my right.

Remy was holding a torch.

The light was flicking on and off.

"More power," I said.

"I do have a theory," Haz said, as we got closer to the car and the garage. "I mean, it's a long shot."

"Go on," I said.

"It is technically possible to save electrics from EMP strikes."

"Nice of you to tell us that *now*," Hannah said.

Haz rolled his eyes. "Not after the event. Before. You can create something called a Faraday Cage. It keeps electrics safe in case of an event like this."

"Yeah," I said. "I remember you saying. My question is... what kind of a person is prepared for this kind of event? Really?"

Haz scratched the back of his neck. "Someone very clever."

"Or someone very paranoid," Remy said.

I was growing more and more confident about taking the car. It drew me towards it, beckoned me inside.

I put a hand on the door.

"Then I think we should—"

"You won't do a bloody thing."

I wasn't sure who the voice came from. And moments later, I realised that's because I didn't know who the voice belonged to at all.

When I turned around, I saw who it belonged to.

There was a man wearing a checkered flannel shirt over a stained white T-shirt. His jeans were baggy and torn. He had long white hair, spindly and brittle. On the top of his head, he wore a flat cap. One of his eyes looked like it was shooting off in another direction.

"Get on your knees. All of you. Now."

And we weren't in a position to argue.

Not when he lifted the shotgun and pointed it at us.

CHAPTER TWENTY-EIGHT

It wasn't long before we were in darkness again.

It was hard to tell whether it was day or night in the room we'd been stuffed inside. The room which, by the way, was barely big enough to fit me, Hannah, Haz, Remy, Sue and her two children inside. We were pressed up against each other, feeling one another shaking. It really was the most terrifying situation I'd ever been in—and I'd been in a few these last couple of days.

As I sat there, nausea crippling my body as the smell of our collective sweat built up, I realised just how awful things were going to get with regards to personal hygiene. I needed a shower, badly, as did everyone else. Rooms like this, or the car, as we'd discussed, were going to end up stinking like mad. It was already hard enough adjusting to the new way of using toilets—which included not flushing because the water supply was just as affected as everything else. Other times, we'd just have to use holes in the ground, then dig over them, things like that.

If everyone started taking this no dignity route—which, soon, they'd be forced to—then things were going to get pretty grim pretty quickly.

But shit. That was the least of our concerns right now.

"I should've stayed back," Sue said. She was by my side, and her children were at her side, crying. Aiden was saying he was scared of the dark, and Sue was trying to reassure him. "I—I should never have followed. I should never have brought my children here."

"You didn't know it was going to play out like this," I said.

"You know, I lost the kids, once. Both of them. Jason and I, we were at a park for the day. It was pretty quiet, except for a few others kids. Anyway, we got chatting to some other parents. And I swear I was watching them. I was watching them at all times. Then they just... I turned around, and they were gone."

"Sounds like something every parent goes through," Hannah said.

"Not like this," Sue said. "I didn't find them that afternoon. I didn't even find them that night. I started to prepare for the worst. I was tearing my hair out. If it wasn't for Jason, I'm not sure I'd ever have made it through."

"What happened?" I asked.

"I don't know," Sue said. "We never found them. They could still be out there."

I frowned. "Wait. But Holly and Aiden are here with you right now."

"I didn't say it was Holly and Aiden that we lost."

Sue looked at me, and although I couldn't make out her face in the darkness, I could tell that she'd just peeled some very painful layers right back. All of a sudden, I understood her fear of losing her children. I understood her paranoia and her pain. I understood her and Jason's urgency to get their children to somewhere safe and not to take any real risks in the quest to do so.

"I'm sorry," I said. "Really. I am."

I pulled against the cuffs around my wrists.

"I'm not going to let any of us get stuck in here forever. That's just not going to happen."

I pulled harder against the metal. I kept on pulling and banging.

"Hey!" I shouted.

"What's he doing?" Haz asked.

"Hey!"

"Scott, he's going to come back here."

"Good," I said. "Good. That's exactly what we want to happen."

I kept on kicking and punching at the wall behind me. The metal echoed as I hit it. Soon, Hannah joined me. And before I knew it, everyone was doing it. Everyone but Sue.

"Trust me," I said. "We're going to get out of here. We're going to—"

The door swung open.

Light flooded into the pitch blackness. I had no idea how long we'd been in here, whether this was another day, but it felt like forever.

The man stood at the opening of the door, shotgun in hand.

"I thought I told you to keep it quiet or I'd kill every one of you?"

"I don't believe you'd do that," I said.

I wasn't sure where my confidence to say that came from. Judging by the terrified look on Haz's face, he didn't either.

"Oh really?" the man said, walking towards me. He pressed the shotgun against my throat. The cold metal made me shiver. But still, I sat upright. I couldn't let my composure break.

"Really," I said. "I think if you were going to kill us, you'd have killed us by now."

There was a pause. And in the man's crooked eyes, I saw thinking. Deliberation.

Then he pulled back the shotgun and cracked it across my face.

"Scott!" Hannah said.

The man lowered down beside me and squeezed my cheeks together. He breathed strangely minty breath into my face. "That was for you trying to steal my car."

Then he let go and reached around my back, and for a second, seeing the knife in his hand now, I thought he was going to stab me.

But he didn't.

Instead, he removed my cuffs.

I pulled my hands in front of me. My wrists were chapped. There was still blood stained on my right hand where the dog had bitten me, but the wound didn't look too bad.

"Up," he said, to each and every one of us, setting us all free. "On your feet."

"Please," Sue begged. "My children. Show mercy. They've been through a—"

"Don't like children. Never have. The sympathy card won't work on me. Now come on. Through here, before I change my mind."

The walk up the steps of the basement—that's what it turned out to be—and into the man's house was daunting because I really didn't know what to expect.

But the first thing I saw when I stepped into his dusty kitchen was even less expected.

A dog.

No. Not just any dog.

The German Shepherd I'd set free. The one that bit my hand.

"Now, if it were up to me, I'd have killed you all. But Lionel here says you saved him from a trap. So I guess you're very lucky to have him fighting your corner."

He put his shotgun to one side and smiled like we were friends all of a sudden, and none of the events that had unfolded mattered at all.

"Um, yeah. He..."

"I'm Derek," he said. "Derek Hooper."

He held out a hand and shook at the air.

"And you are?"

"Oh," I said. "I'm Scott. This is Hannah. Remy. Haz. Sue. Sue's two children, Holly and Aiden."

Derek looked at and studied each of them. "Pleasure to meet you. Pleasure to meet you all."

He turned and walked down the corridor, out of his kitchen and into a long hallway.

"Um," I said. "Aren't you forgetting something?"

He turned and frowned. "Forgetting what?"

"You just had us locked away in your basement for... well, I don't know how long. And now you're just letting us free?"

He chuckled, then waved a hand at me. "Oh, I know you kids aren't a threat. You just needed teaching a lesson." He said it like we were nothing more than annoying ten-year-olds that needed a telling off.

"The power," Hannah said, stepping forward. "The car. How does it have power? How does your torch have power?"

Derek smiled like he was happy someone had finally asked the question. "Follow me. You'll find out."

We all looked at one another. I felt like I was Alice being led down the rabbit hole. Or a kid being offered candy by a stranger. I wasn't sure which felt worse.

Still, I took a deep breath, and I followed.

When I reached the room that Derek was looking into, I couldn't understand at first. I couldn't *comprehend* what I was seeing.

"You heard of preppers?" Derek asked.

"In America," I said. "I didn't know..."

"Well, this is good ol' Blighty, my friend. And I'm a prepper."

I looked around at the three guns. I saw the fishing rods, the nets, the traps that had been set up. And I saw a little metal cage, which had a watch inside it.

That watch was ticking.

"Now come on," he said, closing the door. "You lot look like you could use a good meal."

Prepper or no prepper, nutcase or no nutcase, a good meal was an offer I couldn't refuse.

CHAPTER TWENTY-NINE

As a part-time vegetarian, I never thought I'd be so thrilled to tuck into a juicy piece of venison.

Alas, a lot had changed in the space of a few days.

It was late, and we sat around the table lit by candlelight. Although Derek insisted he had enough working lights to keep this place lit up, he didn't want to draw too much attention to himself, or to any of us, which was admirable, really. Instead, the curtains were sealed shut, and beyond the curtains, wooden boards were pressed up against the windows, keeping any light from escaping.

It also meant that anyone could be out there, watching, which made the hairs on my arms stand on end.

It was windy outside, and I could hear it creaking the foundations of this old house. The light from the candles was dim, and it felt like we were some kind of medieval family tucking in for a feast.

Everyone was silent when they ate. Well, not *silent*. They were gorging on food, of course. We all were. But we weren't speaking. We were just too focused on the energy source in front of us, reduced to our base instincts.

When I'd finished, feeling full, I sat back and held the glass of red wine Derek had poured for me.

"Let me guess," I said. "You caught the deer yourself?"

Derek grinned. "Bingo."

"How do you do a thing like that?"

"It's not so hard when you have some guns in your possession. But yeah. The preparation has to be done carefully. A deer goes a long way, though. You can cook the meat right away. You can dry some of it in the sunlight and treat it as jerky. The hunting's the easy part, really."

I lifted my hand, which Derek had bandaged. "Evidently."

We laughed, all of us. As we ate some more and drank some more wine, I could sense the collective spirits of this place lifting. The children seemed happy to finally be around a table. Sue... she looked distant, and grief-stricken, and kept bursting into tears, but she couldn't be blamed for that. Not when her husband's death was still so recent, still so raw.

Hannah leaned over to me, reached for the bottle of wine. When she lifted it back, she spilled a little onto my lap.

"Oops," she said.

She put a hand on my leg, and I flinched. But then I let it rest there. I looked into her eyes, smelled the wine on her breath, and found myself growing intoxicated with her.

Then I cleared my throat, and Hannah moved her hand away, and the moment was forgotten, just like that.

"Don't you think about him?" I asked.

She topped up her wine. "Think about who?"

"Your boyfriend. Don't you wonder how he's doing?"

She sighed and sipped back some of her wine. "Sometimes. But mostly I don't bother because I know he'll be doing just fine."

"You sure about that?"

She looked into my eyes, and I felt like there was something unrevealed about her boyfriend. Something she didn't want to say, at least not in words. "Trust me," she said. "He's well suited for this world."

I didn't think of that as a negative. But the way Hannah said it... well, I wondered how she'd intended for it to be taken after all.

"So I'm assuming you guys are heading for the coast?" Derek said, breaking his silence.

I frowned. "What's at the coast?"

"Over Blackpool way. There should be a military camp. Imagine they've got a view to getting people out of here."

"Wait," Remy said. "How do you know this?"

"Old radio in the garage," he said. "I heard it. Must've... must've been just before the EMP hit."

"So you're saying the military knew this was going to happen?"

"I don't for a second doubt it," Derek said. "My theory is either solar flare, which turned out being stronger than expected. Fried a few satellites on its way down, things like that. Either that or an EMP attack from one of the the many rich, volatile governments who hate the west. Our government might've got intelligence that something bad was about to happen, and set the ball rolling. But by the time that EMP was ready to explode, it was already too late."

"If it is a weapon," I said. "Then that means there will be other countries out there willing to come in and take us out of here—or at least send people in to work on getting things back in order. Right?"

Derek lowered his glass. "That's part of what I'm worried about. The fact we haven't seen any evidence of outsiders at all... maybe it's just that they don't want to send planes or helicopters over a zone where an EMP has just gone off. But maybe it's because..."

He stopped and wiped his lips.

"Because what?" I asked.

"If a solar flare fried the Earth hard enough... then there's a chance this isn't an isolated incident. There's a good chance it's the whole damned world that's affected."

I took a few seconds to take that in. I'd heard Haz hypothesising about that possibility a while back, but I didn't for a second believe it could be true.

"What then?" Hannah asked.

"If that's the case," Derek said. He paused, just for a few seconds, deep in thought. "Well, we'd better get topped up on wine, 'cause we're in for a hell of a bumpy ride!"

He poured himself some more wine. The rest of us topped up our glasses. I was starting to feel pretty drunk and beyond caring, and saw quickly how alcoholics let themselves be caught up in booze as a way of self-medicating away the world's problems.

"To the end of the world!" Derek said, in a way that could easily have been interpreted as nihilistic but instead rang devastatingly true.

I lifted my glass. As did everyone else. "To the end of the world."

We clicked our glasses.

We'd investigate the military camp that Derek had told us about over at the coast.

But for now, all we could do was drink.

CHAPTER THIRTY

Garry looked through the trees at the house in the darkness and he heard the clinking of glasses and laughter from inside.

He was cold. He was exhausted. By his side, the same two people as before, Mitch and Peter, as well as a couple of others who had joined them since. They were on the same page as each other, though. They understood that this world was theirs for the taking, so that's exactly what they were going to have to do from now on.

Take.

Take.

Take.

Garry took a deep, shaky breath. His stomach cried out with hunger when he smelled the food. He'd been following the group for a long time, ever since they'd left the suburbs, where he'd killed that man called Jason.

There'd been a few moments where he'd nearly been seen. In fact, he swore at one stage that one of the kids looked right into his eyes.

But he just put a finger over his mouth and descended into the grass.

"So are we gonna just wait here while they're cooking something delicious or are we actually gonna do something about them?" Mitch asked.

Garry gritted his teeth together. His first proper meal since release from prison. Of course, he'd eaten things over the last few days. Snack bars he'd taken from the hands of people he'd beaten up. He had quite a few decent supplies to get him by, seeing as it didn't look like the electricity was returning anytime soon. And that was something he was okay with. After all, the return of electricity meant that he would be on a list of escaped convicts. The government would have to try and get everyone back inside, starting with the most dangerous first.

But hell. He didn't envy their job. Maybe they'd just hit a reset, unable to round everyone up. Maybe they'd offer amnesty to those who didn't offend again. It'd cause problems. There'd be tension in the air, protests in the streets.

But that was a long way to be thinking ahead. After all, right now, he was living in a world without rules, and he was making the most of it while it stayed this way.

And he longed for a cooked meal.

"We wait," Garry said.

Mitch sighed. "Wait? We've been waiting this whole damned journey. I mean, the guy has a car, for God's sakes. We can take it right now and get out of here."

Garry remembered the way the man looked him in the eye. He was the first person who'd looked him in the eye, without fear, for as long as he could remember. Everyone inside feared him. Even the prison officers.

And everyone he'd run into outside had feared him, too. He'd made that so.

But this man...

"Maybe we won't have to take the car," Garry said.

He looked at Mitch, and in the darkness, he smiled.

He knew Mitch understood.

He looked back at the house and listened to the chatter of conversation fill the air.

It was so perfect.

So beautiful.

He tightened his grip on the knife.

He couldn't wait to destroy the serenity.

CHAPTER THIRTY-ONE

I was in the middle of my best night's sleep in a long, long time when a sudden bang woke me up.

I jolted upright, gasping for air. The darkness around me was intense and disorienting. I knew right away where I was—in Derek's place, in one of the spare bedrooms. It was a large old cottage, so he had plenty of room to share with us.

For a moment, as I sat there gasping, the taste of sweat on my lips, I wondered if the bang I'd heard was something in my dreams. After all, it was entirely possible. It wasn't out of the question that I should be a bit jumpy with everything going on; a little bit on edge.

I sat there for a few seconds in the darkness, listening for any other sounds.

When I didn't hear a thing, I took a few deep breaths and leaned back onto my pillow. It was damp with my sweat. Whatever I'd been dreaming, it must've been intense. Stress dreams were something I just had to put up with. I ground my teeth when I was anxious, and obviously I didn't have my dentally crafted bite guard with me, which wasn't just going to be a pain for the people around me, but in the long run was going to cause me serious tooth problems.

That new problem reached the forefront of my mind, threatening to keep me awake.

Then I heard another bang.

This time, I sat right up. My heart pounded. My skin tingled.

I'd heard a bang. No doubt about it.

I couldn't be sure what it was, only that I swore it was coming from downstairs.

I listened to that bang once again. It sounded like someone was trying to break in. Was I the first to hear the bang? What did I do about it?

I decided the only real course of action was to get out of bed and see for myself.

I walked as steadily as I could across the room, towards the door. The darkness was suffocating. I had a little torch with me, though, one that Derek had kept in his many Faraday cages. I didn't want to use it, though. I wanted to keep darkness on side until I was absolutely certain what was going on here.

I reached the door and pushed it open. It creaked, noisy in the night.

"Derek?" I whispered as I stepped out into the corridor.

Another bang against the front door.

Somewhere downstairs, a growl. Lionel.

I walked to the top of the stairs and I saw the door moving.

Someone was trying to break in here.

No doubt about it. Someone was trying to get in.

I clenched my fists. I took another few steps towards the top of the stairs.

Then I felt a hand on my arm.

I leapt up so much that I almost tripped and fell down the stairs.

"Hey," a voice said. And after a few seconds, I realised I knew that voice.

"Hannah," I said, trying my best to hide my embarrassment of my terrified reaction. At least it was dark. "Don't make me jump like that."

"Never mind you jumping," another voice said. It was Derek, this time. And it soon became clear to me that everyone was standing on the landing area, now. Remy. Haz. Sue, and her two children. Even Lionel had come upstairs to join us. "Most important thing here is we get to the safe room."

"The safe room?" Hannah said.

"The room with all the weapons and supplies," Derek said as if it was just common knowledge and Hannah was asking a stupid question.

"But those people," Sue said. "They're going to get in here."

"Maybe so," Derek said, walking to the top of the staircase. "But they aren't gonna get much further than the front door when we're armed to the brim. Now come on."

He started walking down the stairs. We all followed him, one by one. It seemed like he was moving steadily, like he didn't want to bring attention to himself. I couldn't help worrying about that door. It sounded like it was going to cave in any second now.

"Shouldn't we get a move on?" I asked.

"Yes," Derek said. "We should. So hurry yourselves up, and make sure you're ready for—"

Derek's voice was interrupted then.

The door slammed off its hinges.

We stood there at the bottom of the stairs, all of us huddled behind Derek. There was a pause as the light from the stairs peeked into the house.

At the door, five silhouettes.

I swore I could see things—weapons, like knives and wrenches and hammers—in their hands.

"Well, well," a voice said, and it was a voice I swore I recognised. "We meet again."

I didn't register who it was. Not then. It'd be a while before I realised that it was the prisoner I'd come head to head with way back in the suburbs. The one who'd killed Jason.

Right now, all I registered was the fact that they were in the house.

They had the weapons.

They had the advantage.

"Get to the safe room," Derek muttered.

I frowned. "What?"

"You heard me. There's no way we're gonna defend this place if all of us run now. The code's 6-4-5-2. And yes, the lock's surge-protected too, in case you're wondering. So get there. Now."

I didn't like the way Derek was talking. "What about you?"

The men started to walk inside the house towards us.

Derek smiled, a look of defeat on his face. "A captain always goes down with his ship."

"But everything you know and—"

"Get to the safe room. And whatever you do, look damned well after my dog. Go. Now!"

I turned around then, and I ran. Remy ran with me. As did Hannah, Haz, Sue and her kids.

I didn't look back to see Derek. I just scrambled by the door, inputting the numbers with my shaky hands.

6-4-5-2.

Shit. I'd missed the "2". A red flash. Needed to be steadier.

I took a breath then I tried again.

6-4-5-2.

This time, a green light flashed. The door clicked.

I went to turn the handle when I looked back at Derek.

He was on his knees. He was facing us now. One of the men had a hammer raised above his head.

Beside me, Lionel whined.

"You can run," the man behind Derek said. "But you can't hide."

I wanted to go over there and help Derek. I wanted to save him.

But I knew from the look on his face that it was already too late.

Two of the people were stepping around him, rushing towards us.

I wasn't armed yet. None of us were.

"I'm sorry," I said, looking Derek in the eye. "I'm so sorry."

Derek looked at me and then at Lionel, a tear rolling down his cheek. "You be a good lad, Lionel. You be a good lad."

I saw the hammer slamming down towards Derek, and I closed my eyes.

Then I stepped inside the room, slammed the door shut, and sunk back into the darkness once again.

Lionel whined as the hammer came down on Derek a second time.

And after that second thump of the hammer, there was silence.

CHAPTER THIRTY-TWO

We backed up against the wall right at the back of the safe room and listened to the men start to bang on the door.

It was so dark in here, redefining what we understood darkness to be. It could be any time of day, but we knew it was still the thick of night because we hadn't been in here for long. Outside, I kept on hearing that banging on the door, and it flinched me out of my trance and back into the everyday reality.

But in the spaces between the banging, I disappeared back into that haze, which was filled with one thing.

The image.

The image of seeing that man, with the hammer, standing behind Derek.

Seeing Derek on his knees like something out of some kind of snuff film or ultra-gritty television show.

And the sounds...

No. I didn't want to think about the sounds. I couldn't let myself. After all, thinking about those sounds just made the whole thing seem all the more real.

"Scott?"

It was Hannah. She was right by my side. Beyond her, I could hear Sue and the children crying. Further along, Lionel, growling and whimpering as he grieved for his fallen companion.

"Scott?" Hannah said. "We need to decide."

I looked at her. "Decide what?"

"What we're going to do."

I understood what she was saying right away. I could fully interpret it. She was suggesting we did something. Fought back. After all, we were in a safe room; a room filled with all kinds of weapons that we could defend ourselves with.

But fighting back with weapons?

Even contemplating using weapons to defend ourselves?

No, worse. To *attack*?

That wasn't the sort of thing that we were supposed to run into. It wasn't the kind of problem that normal upstanding citizens like me and Hannah and everyone here were supposed to have on our plate.

This was the sort of thing that experts dealt with. That people in armies, and in gangs, had on their plate.

Not web design workers. Not sociology students.

"That door's not gonna hold forever," Remy said.

"It might," Haz said.

"Doesn't matter how strong it is," Sue said. "We can't just stay holed up in here forever. I mean, there's supplies. There's stuff we could get by on. But not forever."

I looked across the room at where Sue was. I was both scared and impressed to be hearing what she was saying. It was quite a turn, from a woman who had previously expressed such reluctance, such fear, to get involved and on board with what we were doing, with what we *had* to do.

But now she was suggesting something even I was uncomfortable with.

"And he huffs, and he puffs," a voice called. I heard that chuckling, and I knew whose the voice was. I knew Hannah probably realised who it was, too. I just wasn't sure whether I wanted to tell Sue whether this was the man who'd killed her husband. I wasn't sure if it would aid us in any way, not really.

It might just make us all the more reckless.

I stood up then, realising that we only had one choice.

I stepped in front of the rest of the group. I flicked on the little blue torch; one of the ones Derek had kept in his Faraday cage.

I moved it across each and every one of the rest of us, then back up at the wall.

"It's not something I want to do. It's something I'm... hell, I'm *scared* about doing. But Sue's right. We can't just stay trapped in here. Not forever."

As I scanned the torchlight against the walls—the little contraptions Derek had created, and most importantly, the three guns—I knew for a fact that everyone was going to be on the same page as me, now.

"We need to stand together," I said, walking over to that smaller handgun—the brand of which I wasn't sure about. I didn't even know how to load one of these things besides what I'd seen in the movies.

"We need to fight," I said.

And then Remy stood up and took the second gun.

There was a pause over the third gun. But in the end, it was Hannah who stepped forward and took it.

We stood together, the guns in hand. It didn't matter so much that we didn't know how to use them. What mattered more was the fact that we were going to look much stronger, much more assertive, much more powerful with these weapons in hand.

I stood at the door. Hannah and Remy were beside me.

We tumbled back a little when another bash hit the door.

"Open up! Open up now!"

I looked at Remy, then at Hannah.

"Ready?" I asked.

They nodded.

And then Sue switched off the light and turned the handle.

What happened next was a blur.

We opened the door, and immediately, Sue shone the bright light into the eyes of the man standing nearest.

Then in that moment of confusion—which surely even these men didn't expect to happen—we pointed our guns at them and stepped out towards them.

"Whoa!" one of them said, backing off. "Whoa. There's no need to—"

"Back off," Remy said. "Right this second."

I saw the blood in the hallway, then. I saw a body. I didn't have to look closely at it to know it was Derek's.

"We can come to some sort of agreement here," the man's voice said.

"There's only one agreement we're going to come to. You're going to back away—"

The next part was even more of a blur.

One of the men grabbed my left arm. He tightened his grip on it.

And in that blurred, muddled moment that ran at no speed at all, I pointed the gun at him and I fired.

The sound was electrifying. The blast made my ears ring. It felt like life changed, right then. Life before the shot was fired and life after.

I didn't realise what was happening until I saw the man falling slowly to the floor. His eyes were wide, reflecting in the bright glimmer of the torchlight. He was looking down at his stomach, which was bleeding. Everyone around him looked shocked, too. Even the people beside me.

When he hit his knees, he gasped for a few seconds. He tried to say something, tried to get something out.

But then, he just looked back up at me with such fear, such disbelief.

"Monster," he said. "You... monster."

His eyes rolled back, then. He fell backwards, onto the floor of the hallway.

And at that moment, as the rest of the people fled, Remy and Hannah pointing their guns at them, I looked down at the body and I knew.

I knew the man was right.

I knew what I'd become.

Monster.

CHAPTER THIRTY-THREE

I looked down at the two bodies lying in the earth and I felt a wave of nausea take hold of me.

It was morning. The clouds were thick, and the rain was falling heavily. We were outside in Derek's garden, which was mostly made up of long, overgrown grass and various contraptions all around the place. There were a few sheds, which were on the verge of collapse, propped up by long, thick beams of wood.

As run down as this place was, it was clear to see that it was Derek's pride and joy. He cared a lot about his home.

So much so that he'd died protecting it.

I looked down at him lying there in the earth. He was six feet under, thereabouts. A couple of the others had suggested we bury him and the man I'd shot together, but I wasn't comfortable with that. They deserved their own graves. Their own resting places.

Derek, in particular, after everything he'd done to defend this place.

I felt a hand brush my arm, and it made my jump. When I looked to my left, I saw that it was Hannah.

She half-smiled at me, grey-faced. "You okay?"

I gripped the shovel in my hand and nodded, but of course I

wasn't. I felt sick. I knew that, for as long as I lived, that smell of the damp earth would remind me of what I'd done.

Of what I was now.

"I'm fine," I said.

"You need a hand digging—"

"No," I said, sternly. "Thank you. But no. I need to do this myself."

Hannah opened her mouth, looking like she was about to protest.

Then she sighed and nodded. "Okay," she said. "Just as long as you know you did what you had to do."

You did what you had to do. That's what everyone kept saying. But they didn't know the truth. They couldn't be inside my head when I'd reacted at that moment.

All I knew was this man had reached out for me. He'd grabbed my arm. For all I knew, he was just trying to get me to lower my weapon, using the only way he saw feasible.

I'd reacted purely out of fear.

"Maybe I didn't have to," I said, not wanting to mope but unable to stop the guilt crippling me.

"You can't say that," Hannah said. "You did the only thing you saw right at that moment."

"We could've negotiated."

"They killed Derek."

I heard Hannah's words clearly this time. And when she looked at me, I knew she didn't feel any guilt about what I'd done. But then again, why would she?

She hadn't pulled the trigger.

"I just…" I started, feeling my throat begin to swell up and wrap around my words.

"It's okay," she said. "You can get it off your chest."

I sniffed and turned away from her, from the hole in the ground in front of me. "I want to just be myself. I don't—I don't want to be this person. I *can't* be that person. Because it's not who I am."

Hannah squeezed my arm a little tighter. "Scott, none of us are the people we used to be. Our identities aren't fixed. One event like this, sure, it can change everything. But it doesn't make you a bad man. It doesn't make you a villain. You did what you thought was right. And besides. We're safe now."

She said those three words with little conviction. I knew she didn't believe them, not really, and neither did I.

"You finish off here," she said. "Then come meet the rest of us. We'll talk."

I smiled at her as the rain poured down from above, trickling down my face. "Thank you," I said.

"Stay strong."

She walked away, and she left me alone with Derek, who I felt partly responsible for, as I dug my shovel into the earth and began to cover him.

Beside the grave, Lionel lay with his head on his paws and began to whimper.

THIRTY MINUTES OR SO LATER, I walked away from the grave I'd dug for Derek and joined the rest of the group around the front of the house, Lionel by my side.

It was Haz who saw me first. He lifted a hand and waved, and then the rest of them turned and faced me, looking at me like I was some kind of ill school kid returning for the first time, trying to act welcoming and accommodating while secretly not wanting to be anywhere near in case they caught some of whatever was in my system.

"Hey," Hannah said, as I walked up to them. "How're you—"

"I've thought about staying here, but truthfully, I think we owe it to Derek to make the most of his supplies and begin our journey."

"Our journey where?" Sue asked.

I took a deep breath. "The military safe zone that Derek told us about. The one by the coast."

Haz shook his head. "Can't help feeling nervous about that idea. We saw what the military did the last time we got near them."

"That was there. We can't judge everyone based on that. It can't be the same everywhere. There has to be something in what Derek said. We have to have faith. Otherwise... well, we just stay here, and then what? We just wait until the day we run out of supplies? We give up? No. That's not what we do. That's not who we are."

I saw the looks on the faces of Sue, of Remy, Hannah, Haz, and Sue's kids.

I pointed back at the house. "In there, there are things that can help us. Things we can use to aid what we're trying to do."

"A lot to learn," Remy said.

"Well, no better time to start learning than the present."

"And you're sure this is the right call?" Sue asked.

I realised then—the questions I was having posed at me—all of it was adding to my credentials as some kind of leader. I'd never been a leader. I'd always been in the background. I didn't think I could be a leader.

Someone had to be. And it looked like that was going to be me.

"I can't be sure," I said. "But I am sure about one thing. If we don't do this—if we don't try—we're going to regret it for the rest of our lives."

I saw Hannah walk towards me. Then Remy. Then Haz, and Sue, and her kids.

"So what do you say?" I asked. "The safe zone. We're all agreed that's where we go. Okay?"

I saw the smiles. I saw the nods.

"We're with you," Hannah said.

I looked over my shoulder at the hole in the ground where the man I'd shot lay.

Then I looked at the hole where Derek was and remembered that cracking sound I'd heard—the first of two moments that I knew would never leave me, not ever.

I looked down at Lionel. "And are you ready, boy?"

He looked back up at me and let out a little bark.

I took that as a yes.

It was time for us to make our way to that safe zone, once and for all.

CHAPTER THIRTY-FOUR

We'd been walking for two days and exhaustion was well and truly starting to catch up with us.

The sky was grey, thick with clouds. It'd been like that for the bulk of our journey. We'd spent a lot of time walking between suburbs, trying to divert clear of them before we could step inside them. As we had things—supplies from Derek's safe room—we didn't want to draw too much attention to ourselves.

That said, there were a lot of people around who had the same idea of moving out of the suburbs because of the chaos of the cities spreading there, so it wasn't like we were alone or anything like that. We encountered someone new pretty much every hour.

But fortunately for us, despite a few frosty moments that could've got nasty, things seemed to be going okay. We hadn't had anything stolen, and we hadn't lost anyone else.

Not yet.

We hadn't taken the car from Derek's quite simply because there wasn't enough fuel in it to get it running. And besides, as much as we could use fuel from other cars, we didn't want to draw attention to ourselves. We knew what was the priority here—

getting to that safe zone. If we could get there as quickly as possible, we wouldn't even have any need for a car.

We had to think long term. We had to be careful.

Hannah put her hands on her knees and leaned forward as we reached the end of a field. She turned and shook her head. Her lips were chapped, and she looked pale.

"You okay?" I asked.

"Blisters on my feet are hurting like a bitch."

"Want a massage?"

"Ew," she said. "No thanks."

"I was joking."

"I should hope so." She stood up again then. The rest of the group passed us, carried on their walk forward. "Hey. How're you holding up?"

I swallowed a lump in my throat and tried to shake off what Hannah said right away. "I'm fine."

"You sure? It's just—"

"I'm fine. Really."

She didn't look convinced. I couldn't blame her for being that way.

But she just said, "Good. Because what you did back at the house..."

"Was the only way," I interrupted. "Right."

Again, Hannah looked like she wanted to push me to speak some more. But she wasn't going to get a thing else from me.

"How much further?" I asked.

Hannah puffed out her lips. "Remy seems to be the directions expert. I'm just the follower."

I nodded, then stepped forward to the stile, crossing over into another field.

"Hey," Hannah said.

I stopped. Looked at her. "What?"

"Do you really..."

"Do I really what?"

"It doesn't matter."

"No. It does matter. What were you going to say?"

"It's just... this talk of a safe zone. I'm not sure I believe it."

Hannah's words vocalised my own thoughts and fears this entire journey. "Derek is... was a clever man. If he says he heard something, then I'd wager a bet he did."

"But it's been days. Do you really think there's going to be something there? I mean, who's to say it won't just be another place that has closed the doors to everyone from the outside, like the bunker back near Sue's old place?"

Sickliness grew in my body, stretching right up through to my chest when Hannah spoke those words. After all, they were my fears too. She wasn't alone in her uncertainties.

But I took a deep, sharp inhalation of breath and smiled. "We won't know what's waiting for us if we give up. So as far as I see it, we've no choice but to press on. Okay?"

A look of uncertainty on Hannah's face. Then a resigned shrug and a smile. "Okay."

"Good." I offered a hand.

She looked at it like it was something filthy. "I can walk without someone holding my hand. Thanks."

I walked ahead, past Lionel—who seemed to be settling into our company pretty happily—before I had to face up to any more embarrassment.

We walked on, much further. Rain fell heavily now, making the mud squelch beneath our feet. Holly and Aiden were playing in the mud, which made Sue smile for the first time since Jason had died. Haz walked with Lionel for the most part, a match made in heaven it seemed.

Remy walked alone, right at the front of the group.

There was something that intrigued me about Remy. It struck me that, in spite of how long we'd all been together now, there was still so little I knew about him.

There was a time for everything.

And now felt like the time to learn who Remy really was.

I caught him up and smiled. "How we progressing?"

He studied the fields like he could tell just from a glance where we were at and what we had to do next. "I'd say we'll be there in a few hours. Hopefully before nightfall."

"And if we don't get there before nightfall?"

"Then we continue tomorrow."

Remy's answers were matter of fact, and hard to take for anything other than their base value. I was finding it hard to start a conversation, especially with the big elephant in the room about his past that was annoying me.

"I know you'd like to know more about me."

I frowned. Remy's words had caught me by surprise. I felt like he was reading my mind. "What?"

Remy half-smiled. "I see the way you look at me. The curiosity. You want to know my past. Don't you?"

I scratched the back of my neck and thought about trying to lie my way around it. But in the end, it felt like honesty was the best policy. "I can't lie. It'd be nice to know something about you. Starting with why you were in the elevator with Julia at my workplace. Or my *old* workplace, I guess."

Remy chuckled like he was enjoying his lack of transparency and the effect it was having on others. "You know I'm in the alternative medicine business."

"So what was a guy in the alternative medicine business doing in my workplace? That's my question."

He looked at me, then. And I felt like he was seeing inside of me, the first person to do so for a long time. "Julia."

My stomach sank when he said her name. "What about Julia?"

"She thought you could use some help in work."

My cheeks flushed. I didn't know what to say. "What?"

"Julia saw the effect losing your mother and your wife had on you. She figured it would help you get back to your best if you had someone come in and talk to you. Someone to train you in meditation, mindfulness, that sort of thing. I was supposed to be sitting in on your interview to monitor your situation."

The explosion of guilt was paralysing. I was literally speechless for a few seconds. "Julia?"

"Julia."

"Julia Wilkinson?"

"That's the one."

"But she hated me."

Remy shrugged. "Sometimes there is a fine line between love and hate."

My desire to know more about Remy evaporated at that moment. All that seemed to matter was the act of kindness Julia prepared for me, especially for that day. So she must've been planning on giving me the job after all. She must've seen just how much I was really struggling.

And I'd left her behind.

I was about to ask Remy more when I saw someone up ahead.

It was a woman. She had short, black curly hair and was wearing a maid's outfit like someone from another century. She was smiling at us, practically beaming. She gave me the creeps.

Then she opened her hands. "Welcome to your salvation," she said. "You made it!"

CHAPTER THIRTY-FIVE

It turned out the woman wasn't from the safe zone after all.

But she had food on the table, and we were all sitting around it now darkness had fallen, rain hammering against the windows, wind creaking the foundations of the house.

The woman was called Margery. Her husband, Bill. He was a plump man with a balding head. He had these brown eyes and this flat smile that didn't seem like it really connected with you when you looked at it; more looked *through* you.

It unnerved me. But again, food was on the table, and this pair was offering shelter.

The dinner table was large and candlelit. Funnily enough, there weren't any light bulbs in the house. The lights were emptied of bulbs, and wax had trickled down the sides of the candles, which made me wonder if perhaps this family didn't use electricity at all, relying on the light of candles to get by. If you'd told me people like this existed a couple of days ago, I'm not sure I would've believed you.

But right now, after having seen Derek's prepper lab and everything else along the way, I was pretty much ready to buy into anything.

The weirdest thing about Margery and Bill's home? The young girls, sitting around the table.

There were five of them, and all of them were dressed in the same white nighties. They looked too young to be Margery's children, and yet Bill looked a lot younger than Margery himself. Perhaps they were grandchildren. Relatives, of some kind.

Whatever they were, the longer this situation dragged on, the more uncertain I got.

But damn, the stew was good.

"So," I said, seeing the need to cut through the awkward silence. "How've you been coping so far?"

Margery frowned. "Coping?"

"The blackout. The EMP strike or whatever it is. How've you been getting on?"

She glanced at Bill, and Bill glanced back at her like the pair of them didn't know anything about what was going on.

Then it dawned on me...

"Wait," I said. "You do realise there's been an event, don't you?"

"What kind of event?" Margery asked.

"A blackout," Haz cut in, eager to explain. "Well, not exactly a blackout. More an EMP strike. It's fried the electricity. Could be country-wide, could be global. Could be... can I just say, this stew is delicious?"

Margery chuckled. "Oh, don't thank me," she said, patting Bill's arm. "Thank the girls, here. Those are the ones you should be grateful to."

Haz looked at them and nodded. A couple of them giggled childishly, even though they had to be in their late teens or early twenties.

This entire dinner was getting weirder by the second.

"So," Hannah said, dipping some crusty bread into her stew. "What you're trying to say is, you're self-sustainable anyway, or something?"

"Off the grid, well and truly," Margery said. "And we have been that way for the best part of a year now."

Lionel looked up at the table hopefully, eager for more scraps.

"Timed that right," Hannah said.

Margery frowned like she didn't really get the reference. Then, when Bill laughed a little, she started laughing too as if she'd just realised Hannah was telling a joke all along.

"And this safe zone we hear about," Remy said. "I'm assuming you won't know much about that, then?"

"Oh, safe zones," Margery said, topping up her glass of wine. "That's what they tell you, isn't it? That's what they promise you. But really, dear, nowhere is safe. Not when it's in the eyes of the government. Not when they are spying on you, putting poison in your food and trackers in your skin."

Everyone went silent. It was clear now that Margery and Bill were the kind of paranoid, tin-foil hat types that would flourish in a world like this.

"Mummy, I hate this."

Aiden's voice cut through the silence, puncturing the atmosphere like a pin to a balloon.

Bill's head swung around, and for a moment, just a fleeting moment, I saw a glimmer of sheer disgust in his deep brown eyes as he looked judgmentally at Aiden.

"I'm sorry," Sue said, clearly embarrassed. "We're really grateful for the food. Really. Aiden's just a fussy eater."

"No he's not," Holly cut in. "You always say it's *me* that's the fussy eater. Remember?"

Sue looked between her children like she was caught between a rock and a hard place. Margery and Bill looked like they'd been personally insulted. I was growing keen to get out of this place as quickly as possible, even if it meant camping out in that storm tonight. Something about this whole setup just didn't ring true, like we were dining on top of an iceberg, unsure of what secrets hid beneath us.

"It's been a long day," I said. "We're all just tired. Truly, though, we're very grateful for your delicious food."

The faith seemed restored to Bill and Margery's faces. They all smiled, and a couple of the girls giggled. "Thank you," Margery said. "You really are such a gentleman. A handsome gentleman, at that. You'd be ideal for Beatrice."

I chuckled a little as the dark-haired girl, Beatrice, made eye contact with me, then looked back down at her food.

"You should try her out."

Bill's voice itself was jarring and disorienting.

So much so that it took a few seconds for the actual contents of his words to make sense in my mind.

"What?" I said.

Bill's eyes were dead set on me now. "You should try Beatrice out. See what you make of her. She's yours if you enjoy each other."

I lowered my fork, feeling my face turn red. Hannah, Remy, Haz, and Sue all looked just as stunned as I was. The children didn't look all that fazed.

Lionel was still looking for fallen scraps.

"I'm sorry," I said, clearing my throat and swallowing a lumpy piece of meat. "I... Do you have a bathroom?"

"I'm sorry if my husband offended you," Margery said. "He's very old-fashioned about these things. Toilet is upstairs, on the far left. We've got a septic tank attached to it, so you should have no problems."

"Thank you," I said, hurrying to my feet.

I felt guilty about abandoning the rest of my friends at the table with that bunch of nutters. I mean, Bill had been pretty clear in what he'd said. Beatrice was *mine* if I wanted her.

And Margery apologised and defended it as an old-fashioned attitude.

Maybe that's all it was. An old-fashioned misogynist.

But still, there was something inherently unpleasant about what I'd been offered. And it made me want to vomit up my food.

I walked up the stairs, past a dressing table. On it, there was a photo of a young couple. They looked vaguely like Margery and Bill, but it must've been taken some years ago.

I made my way up the stairs, then headed for the bathroom.

When I reached the door, I stopped.

There was a noise coming from the room on the right.

My body froze. Part of me wanted to believe they had a pet. That's all it was. Or the wind. The wind was just creaking the house foundations. That had to be it.

I made a move to the bathroom door again when I heard something else.

This time, it was like a mumble.

I turned around, hairs on my arm standing on end. I could hear plates and knives clinking downstairs as everyone continued with their dinner.

I wanted to look in that room.

I wanted to see what the noise was.

But the thought that there could be something in there terrified me.

Still, I took a deep breath. I crept over to the door, being sure to keep glancing downstairs in case anyone came out and caught me.

I put a hand on the handle. Turned it. And as the wind roared and the rain fell heavily, I felt more and more stupid about what I was doing.

When I opened the door, the first thing that hit me was the smell.

The room was dark. The windows were boarded up. Flies buzzed around.

I'd never smelled a decomposing body. I wanted to believe I still hadn't.

But I'd heard and read descriptions of what they were like.

And this was it.

I stepped into the room. I lifted the torch, which I'd kept secret to the hosts, out of my pocket. I could see something on the bed. A mound. I didn't want to know what that mound was.

But I had to know.

I lifted the torch with my shaky hand. Downstairs, I heard more plates clinking. More laughter.

I lifted the torch higher, held my breath as nausea crippled me.

Then, I switched on the light.

When I saw what was on the bed, I couldn't keep my food inside of me for a second longer.

I just knew one thing, for certain.

We had to get out of this place.

We had to get out, fast.

CHAPTER THIRTY-SIX

I walked back into the dining room trying my best to look as calm and collected as I possibly could, especially after what I'd just seen in the upstairs bedroom.

The candlelight of the dining room cast a terrifying glow over the place. When I walked in, it was Bill's eyes which met mine first, and they seemed to have taken on a whole new level of intensity. He looked at me like he was trying to figure out how much I knew; whether I'd gone snooping. Shit. Had I failed to clean some vomit off myself, which I couldn't keep inside me? Was I making it too obvious that I'd just seen something that I hoped I'd never see, and I'm pretty sure nobody else would hope to see, either?

Then Margery interrupted and broke the tension of our stare.

"Scott, my dear. Would you like some dessert?"

I took my seat, sat down in it, but doing so just brought an overwhelming spectre of dread right over me again. "I'm okay. Thanks."

"Are you okay, Scotty-boy?" Haz asked. "You look pretty pale."

"I'm fine."

"Look like you've seen a ghost!" he repeated.

I glared at him. "Really. I'm fine."

I hoped he could tell from the tone of my voice that I wasn't fine. I hoped he'd realise that something was desperately wrong and that I was giving him a cue to prepare for... well, prepare for what exactly?

What could we do?

What options did we have?

"That's a shame," Margery said, scooping up some cake and dishing it out between the guests. "It's fruitcake. My speciality."

"Got that right," Hannah muttered.

"What did you say?" Margery asked.

She smiled and raised a hand. "I said I'd love some, thanks."

As I watched the rest of the meals get served, all I could think about was what I'd seen in that room upstairs.

First the smell.

Then, when I'd switched the torch on...

"You don't look well at all," Margery said. "Would you like me to get you some water? A paracetamol, perhaps?"

"I'd... actually I'd appreciate that. Thanks."

I had no real intention of taking that paracetamol. After all, I could end up just like the people I'd seen in that bedroom.

The couple chained to the bed.

One of them, the man, dead.

The woman, alive, barely.

Margery and Bill weren't who they said they were at all...

I lifted my head as the rest of the table ate, and I saw Bill was staring right at me.

I moved my finger around the trigger of the gun. We'd given up our two other guns when we'd first been welcomed inside, but I'd kept hold of this one. I'd made sure nobody knew that.

I'd already used the gun once and wasn't too pleased about having to use it again.

But I had to, didn't I?

I had to.

"You might as well be honest," Bill said, leaning back and smiling. When he leaned back, I saw he had a little pistol. It might well have been one of our own.

Sue squealed when she saw it, grabbed her kids and held them tight.

"Whoa," Hannah said. "What the hell's going on here?"

"On your feet," Bill said.

"But seriously," Hannah said. "What's—"

"If you ask questions, I'll have you on your feet too. Scott. On your feet. Now."

I felt my hand shaking on the trigger of the gun. I couldn't shoot someone else, could I? I couldn't kill another person.

"Now!" Bill barked.

I stood up. But I kept my hands in my pockets as I stood.

"Hands in the air."

"Seriously," Haz said, looking around for some kind of support that his confusion was justified. "What the hell is going on here?"

"Someone's been looking around where they shouldn't have," Bill said. "And if they'd just behaved... if they'd just gone to the toilet, like a good boy, maybe they'd have made it. Hands in the air. Now!"

I realised then I had no choice.

It was now or never.

I lifted my hands and pointed the gun at Bill.

His daughters—or whoever they were—all five of them, shrieked.

I went to fire.

A shot blasted past Bill's head, smashing the window behind him.

"You bloody bastard..."

He stormed towards me, and I don't know why but I dropped the gun. I raised my hands. "I'm sorry," I said. "I'm sorry. I was just—"

"You smashed our windows. You any idea how much those

windows'll cost to replace?"

The women around the table, all five, looked afraid.

Bill walked towards me, slowly, gun raised.

He stopped right in front of me and kicked my gun away. Then he pushed the gun to my chest and looked at me with those distant, glassy eyes.

"You made a big mistake just then," he said. "A big mistake."

"Bill?" Margery said.

He didn't turn around. Not at first.

"It's Jenny, Bill. She's not in her room."

He turned around then, confusion on his face.

Just for a second, I saw him glance at Margery in misunderstanding.

Then a woman stepped up behind Margery and put a knife to her throat.

The woman I'd uncuffed from the bed without them knowing. Jenny.

"Whoa!" Bill shouted.

I punched him, then. Knocked the gun right out of his hand. I pointed it at him.

"Don't move."

"Wait—"

"Don't move a muscle! Someone—someone grab the other gun."

Nobody moved.

"Someone grab it!"

Remy rushed for it. He stood up, pointed the gun at Bill as he stood beside me.

"Please," Margery mumbled, as Jenny—the woman I'd freed from the room upstairs—held a knife to her neck. "We just wanted a nice dinner with nice people."

Hannah went to help Jenny hold Margery. Haz, reluctantly, kept an eye on the girls around the table, who looked more afraid than anything.

"You killed him, didn't you?" I said to Bill. "You came in here, and you locked that couple up in their own home. You left the man to die. And you'd have left Jenny to die, too. Wouldn't you?"

For the first time, Bill looked at me with a glimmer of normalcy that frightened me.

A smile stretched across his face, tugging at the corners of his mouth. "I did what I had to do. Now you'll do what you have to do."

He looked at the gun, and I knew what he meant.

"No," Margery begged. "Please. Please don't hurt him. Please don't hurt my angel."

Part of me wanted to, for what he'd done to that man I'd found in the bedroom, and for the emaciated figure he'd turned Jenny into.

But another part of me didn't want to kill someone else.

"Turn around," I said.

Bill chuckled. "You can't do it, can you?"

"Just—just turn around."

"You don't have the strength. You can't face up to the ugliness. And that'll get you nowhere."

I tickled the trigger tighter than ever before.

"Please!" Margery begged.

Then I stopped. Because as insane as these people were, they were still just people, and someone else could bring them to justice. I wasn't a self-appointed law. I couldn't—

Then, a gunshot cracked through the room.

For a second, I wondered if my gun had malfunctioned when I realised that smoke was coming from the end of Remy's gun.

A bullet hole drooled blood down the front of Bill's head.

The glassiness returned to his eyes as if he'd just gone back to his normal self.

Then he dropped down to his knees in a heap.

Margery looked on with wide-eyed terror. "No!" she screamed.

But not for long.

Not when Jenny pulled the blade across her throat.

And when she'd pulled that blade, Jenny too fell to her knees herself and collapsed, unconscious.

Silence filled the room. Blood oozed from Bill and Margery's bodies. I shook as I held the gun in my hand, not responsible this time but a part of what had happened, of what I'd witnessed. More of the food crept up my throat as Sue held on to her crying children, covering their eyes, and Lionel cowered in the corner.

I looked around at the five women, pale, shocked in the middle of the table.

"It's okay now," I said. "You... you're free now."

Beatrice made tearful eye contact with me. "But they were our saviours. We... we don't know what to do without them. They were our saviours!"

"You can come with us."

"No!" another of the women screamed. "We won't leave them. We'll never leave them."

As Hannah checked on Jenny, we all stood around and watched as the five women gathered around the bodies of the dead and mourned them.

I wished we could do more for these women. I wished we could at least begin to understand what they'd been through, how long they'd been here, and what they were so afraid of.

But in the end, these people were caught up in their own myths, their own lives. And we couldn't begin to understand what they'd been through, whether this was some kind of cult or whatever, we just couldn't be sure.

"Don't go far," I said, as I walked over the bloodstained carpet. "When we reach the safe zone, we'll send someone here to help you."

"We don't want your help," Beatrice spat.

But in her grief, I could hear nothing but desperation, as we walked out of the dining room, together, away from another bloodbath, all of us changed people all over again.

CHAPTER THIRTY-SEVEN

The sun beamed down from the cloudless sky, and as I inhaled, I felt the scars of last night being cleansed right from my system.

We had been walking since sunrise. We were all tired and exhausted after last night's ordeal with Bill and Margery. To be honest, none of us had really spoken about what had happened. It felt like if we brought it up, it would tear away the scabs that had temporarily formed over our wounded minds.

There was a problem, and the problem was our weapons. We'd searched high and wide for the guns we'd handed over, but they were gone. In the end, we were left with just the two guns and not very much ammo. Nine bullets between us, in fact. But I supposed those nine bullets could be the difference between life and death.

I could tell from the way Remy was clenching his jaw that what he had done troubled him.

But he'd spared me having to kill someone else. I didn't have that on my conscience.

At least, that wasn't the plan.

But of course I did. I was a part of this group. I was a killer; all of us were killers, even if by extension.

Our main concern was Jenny. She had come around not long after her collapse, but she had been severely dehydrated and malnourished. We let her have some of our supplies, but we knew they weren't going to keep her alive forever. She needed medical attention, really. She needed proper food and proper shelter. Walking out here, camping, none of that was going to make her better anytime soon. It was only going to worsen her condition.

Now, we'd stopped in the woods, where I was attempting to cook without using the portable stove or any of Derek's contraptions. Whenever anyone asked me why, I said it's because we might not have those things forever, and that I wanted to be sure I had the knowledge to know what I was doing if I did end up with completely nothing.

I'd curled a small flexible tree sapling into an oval, using the smaller branches as a cord. I'd added some crossbars using leftover branches, the flexible cord letting them slide up and down to suit whatever food was going on it perfectly. That way, I could roast whatever meat or food I found over a pile of coals or an open flame. It was hard work, but I was making progress.

"I can't stop thinking about the look on her face," Hannah said.

Her voice made me jump a little. It seemed weird that she was addressing last night—or at least alluding to it. "Might be better to avoid talking about it," I said.

"No," she said. "I'm better when I talk about things. Gets things off my chest."

"Just a shame for the rest of us who have to hear it."

"Look. What happened last night happened. But I... I can't help thinking if this is just how it is. How things always have been."

I narrowed my eyes. "What're you trying to say?"

"I guess I'm thinking whether we've really changed so much at all. If the world's really changed. Or if this shift has just brought out the worst of us that's always been there, deep down."

I thought about what Hannah was saying. Did I have the capability of killing someone a few days ago? Did I think I could survive in a world where everyone was out for themselves?

No. I didn't.

I couldn't.

I walked over to Hannah and put a hand on her shoulder. "Whatever the case, we're still here. And we're getting closer to the safe zone. When we get there, sure. We'll have memories. Things we'll have to live with for the rest of our lives. Hell, I'll have nightmares. But at least we'll have security. At least we'll have order. And that's the most important thing of all. Right?"

She smiled a little then, and I saw a twinkle in her eye. "I've not been entirely honest with you."

My stomach sank. I didn't know what was coming, but I wasn't sure if it could be good. "What do you mean?"

"Back when we first met," she said, lowering her head. "I told you I was a student."

"Wait. You're not a student?"

"I'm a patient."

I frowned. I couldn't understand what Hannah was saying. "A patient? Like..."

"Not anything physical. But... mentally. I was sectioned three months ago. I lost both my parents in an accident and I... I didn't cope too well."

I saw her holding her wrists like she always did, and suddenly things just clicked into place in an awful way. "Hannah..." I said.

"I wasn't supposed to get too far from the place where I was staying. And it was a nice place, really it was. But I just felt suffocated there. So I... Even though I knew it'd get me in trouble, I caught a train, and I figured I'd see where I ended up."

She shrugged, then.

"And here I am."

We were silent for a while. The rest of the group were quite a way ahead now.

"So the stuff about your boyfriend..."

"All made up."

I nodded. "I'm sorry. About your parents. Really."

She smiled back at me. "I know you are. But weirdly... since all this chaos, I know it sounds completely crazy but... well, I've felt freer than I have in a long, long time. I just worry that when we get to the safe zone—"

"It'll be back to normality, where you'll be judged crazy by the people in charge."

I saw the tears build in her eyes like I'd taken the words right out of her mouth—words I was sure she hadn't said to many people—if anyone.

Then she did something unexpected.

She stepped towards me and hugged me.

I put a hand on her back and hugged her, too. I felt her warmth as she held me close, together in the silence.

"I'm glad I met you," she said.

I felt my jaw quivering and tears of my own beginning to roll down my face. "I'm glad I met you too."

We stood there for a while, holding one another, when Haz stepped back towards us.

"Sorry to interrupt whatever this is," he said. "But you might wanna know something important."

"What?" I asked.

"We've found it," he said, smile on his face. "The safe zone. We've found it."

CHAPTER THIRTY-EIGHT

When I stepped outside the woods and looked down the hill towards the sea, I saw right away what Haz was talking about.

It was a military base of some kind, no doubt about it. It looked like it had been set up pretty recently. There were fences, makeshift tents, all kinds of things like that. There were even green military vehicles parked up and waiting.

There was no sign of life, which disconcerted me and made me wonder. It made tension well up inside me.

But I didn't want to address that right now.

"We're here," Sue said, smiling, tears rolling down her cheeks as the kids jumped up and down beside her. "We're actually here."

We stood there together a little while longer. I hadn't said anything. Neither had Hannah, or Remy or Haz. No doubt, all of us were thinking the same thing. *Hoping* the same thing.

That there would be life inside those tents.

That there would be order inside those tents.

That the nightmare would end inside those tents.

"Well?" Haz said. "No point waiting around. Last one to the safe zone's a big loser!"

I saw Haz attempting to look optimistic as he jogged down the hill towards the safe zone, Lionel chasing after him with his tongue flying everywhere, but I could see he was trying to fool himself. He was trying to put on a front to convince himself that everything would be okay down there. Because everything *had* to be okay down there, didn't it? They'd put all their eggs in one basket, and that basket was right ahead of them.

If the kind of hope they were expecting wasn't there waiting for them... well, I didn't like to think about the other options because I wasn't sure what the other options were besides to try to survive for as long as possible before inevitably starving.

I looked at Hannah. She looked at me.

She held out a hand.

After a few seconds, I took it.

Then, together, we made our way down the hill, towards our safe haven.

The closer we got to it, the more the silence of the place really started to become apparent. We slowed a little because Jenny was still struggling, and she needed all the strength she had, even if she had shown signs that she was getting a little better recently.

As for the silence... well, it wasn't a noticeable difference from anywhere else. After all, silence had been a prevalent thing the last few days.

But the very fact that we were at a safe zone, expecting something other than silence, and weren't being met by any kind of noise...

That, I found, disconcerting.

"We go in together," Hannah said, as we all reached the partly open gates. "We stay close."

"Will they have toys, Mummy?" Aiden asked.

"Will they have other children too?"

Sue looked like she was about to say yes, there would be toys and children and all kinds of joys inside this place.

Then she must've seen the uncertainty on my face because she didn't say anything else.

We slowly walked towards the entrance to the tent. As we got closer, past the vehicles, all empty, I wanted to believe that we were just the first ones here. I wanted to believe that I was just being paranoid after days of searching, days of hope, none of that hope being realised.

I reached the tent. I moved my head close to it, so that I could hear inside.

There wasn't anything to hear.

I closed my eyes then and took a few deep breaths. Just like when I'd reached the upstairs room at Bill and Margery's, I didn't want to look behind this tent entrance because I knew that what was behind it could destroy all the hope I—and everyone here—had.

"Go on," Remy said. "You have to. *We* have to."

I looked from Remy to Sue to Hannah to Haz. Then, I looked at the kids. I hoped for their sakes that there was some kind of hope behind this tent entrance.

Then I moved the tent opening aside and stepped inside.

I walked inside the huge tent. I could see traces that people had been here. Empty crisp packets, discarded. Cigarette stubs. And I could smell humanity in the air too like plenty had been here. Kind of like it was a concert hall that had been full of life not so long ago.

It was empty now.

"Is anyone here?" Sue said. It sounded like she'd tried to shout, but in the end, her voice went to nothing but a weak whimper.

I walked further inside, into the tent.

And when I stepped around the corner, I wished I hadn't.

"Stop," I said, holding up a hand and covering my mouth.

"Scott? What's—"

"Get the kids outside. Now."

I realised then it was too late. Everyone was alongside me. Everyone was looking where I was looking.

There was a gated area.

And behind those gates, a mass of bodies, piled on top of one another.

I felt my bottom lip quiver. I heard Sue scream and more commotion.

I wanted to turn away.

I wanted to run.

Instead, I walked towards that pile of bodies.

The closer I got to them, as white as shop front mannequins, I realised what'd happened to them. They'd been shot. They were mostly clean wounds, right through the heads.

I could see some of the people inside were wearing military gear. And I couldn't know for sure what had happened here. Only that, in the back of my mind, I could still hear the echoes of their screams.

"What happened?" Hannah said, her voice quivery. "How... how can this happen?"

I looked at the body of a young woman, not much older than Hannah.

Then, I saw something in her palm.

I reached down towards her, totally detached now, still cold with shock.

"Scott? What're you—"

"It's a note," I said.

I pulled the note from the girl's cold, solid fingers. I looked into her eyes, so dull and lifeless, such a waste, and for a moment I felt all the hope I'd ever had sinking from my body and turning to liquid.

I looked at the note. Opened it up. Slowly.

And as I read the words, I felt that little hope I had left inside drifting further and further away.

Army were here. Boats came. Some army went bad, no space on boats. Going to kill us. Love you Sam. X

Then, a splatter of blood across the bottom of the note.

"Scott? What's it say?"

I looked at Hannah. Then I looked past her at Jenny, Haz, Remy, Sue and her kids. I wanted to give them good news. I wanted to give them hope.

But all I could do was give them the truth.

"It's over," I said.

Haz narrowed his eyes. "What is?"

I swallowed a sickly, nauseous lump in my throat as the thought of that young girl's dead eyes staring back at me spiralled my mind.

"The safe zone. The hope. Our survival. The old world. All of it. It's... it's over."

CHAPTER THIRTY-NINE

I walked off into the distance, way ahead of the rest of the group.
The afternoon was stretching on. Soon, it would turn into evening, then that evening would turn into night, and darkness would fall once again.

Total darkness. Darkness I knew I wasn't going to escape or be able to conquer.

Darkness that would be in place for as long as I lived, even if the power did somehow miraculously switch back on.

I squinted at the sunlight. I knew I should appreciate it, especially contrasted with how dark it could get in Britain. I looked at its beautiful form shining over the trees, and the towns and suburbs in the distance. Maybe I'd go back to one of those towns. Maybe I'd find a place to stay for a while, to lay down and hide in.

Or maybe I'd just keep on walking, alone.

Because one thing was for sure.

There was no way I could stay with my group. Not now I knew what staying with them meant.

Survival. Biding our time for the next disaster to happen, moving from place to place until the day we inevitably died.

That was life now.

And it was a life I wasn't sure I was ready to face.

I heard voices behind me. Haz, I thought. He was calling me, telling me to wait up. But I wasn't going to slow down, not for anyone. Sure, I'd feel guilty just ditching this group, especially since I had some supplies. Not much good me keeping them anyway, to be honest. What good was I going to be at surviving on my own? I didn't know the things Haz knew. I didn't have the drive Hannah had. I didn't have the calm, collected nature that Remy had. And I didn't have the caring, maternal drive that Sue had.

I was just Scott Harvard, a normal guy, just like most of the rest of the population, and I didn't have what it took.

I tasted sickliness in my throat as I stepped further through the grass and drifted towards the trees. I heard birdsong, and I thought of my Harriet and the times we'd go on walks like this, losing ourselves in the middle of nowhere. So many times in those walks, we'd played out a fantasy that we were walking with two beautiful little twins—a boy and a girl—and that we were each holding their hands, laughing with them, crunching through the leaves with them.

And although I'd realised for a while now that I was never going to have that life, it finally dawned on me, right now, as I walked completely alone.

"Scott!" Hannah called. "Wait up!"

I looked back. I could see the rest of the group jogging towards me, but they were quite a way away.

"I'm sorry," I said, under my breath, swallowing a lump in my throat. "Take care."

And then before they could catch me, I drifted off into the trees, into the nothingness, alone.

CHAPTER FORTY

I wasn't sure how long I ran into the woods, only that I had to keep on going.

I could still hear voices somewhere behind me. They seemed to be getting further and further away, though, which was what I wanted. My feet were sore. My back, even more so, from the pack I had. But more crippling than anything was the guilt I felt for what I was doing.

Running away.

Not facing the problems head on.

Not stepping up, standing naively in the background, just like I'd always been accused of doing.

I ran further, and I thought of my childhood. I thought of school, where I'd never lead groups, rather follow and hope for the best. I remembered my desire to be on the school football team. My obsession with the sport... only not to make it, all because I didn't have the confidence to push myself in the way the other boys did.

I'd missed out on so many things, all because I'd chosen to step into the shadows time and time again rather than emerge into the limelight.

I stopped, then. Suddenly, it didn't seem to matter that I could hear voices or footsteps heading my way. Suddenly, none of that seemed to matter at all.

What mattered was that I was still here.

That little voice in my ear kept on whispering at me telling me to give up, to slip into the background again, to go into hiding because that's all I was, really—a hider. A quitter. A faker. I was worthy of nothing and no one, so I was just to fall back into oblivion and leave the world to do its thing around me.

But for the first time in a long time—maybe even the first time in my life—I found myself standing there, breathing deeply, and saying the word: "No."

Just saying that word liberated me, in a sense. I wasn't sure how to describe it other than I felt a weight lifting from my shoulders, rising into the sky above.

"No."

And right away, as I stood in the middle of the trees, sweat pouring down my face, heart racing, I felt the weight of that one word building up in meaning.

No, I was not giving up.

No, I was not running away.

No, I was not going to abandon the people I'd worked so hard to bond with; the people I'd fought so hard to unite.

Instead, I was going to stand up; I was going to take some responsibility, and I was going to fight.

For what?

For our survival.

I turned around and saw Hannah and Remy running through the trees, Lionel by their side, clearly enjoying the exercise.

"Scott?" Hannah said. "What the hell are you doing?"

I thought about lying, but then I realised there was no better option than the truth in times like these. "I was running."

"Running?" Hannah said, struggling to get her breath back. "Running from what?"

I swallowed a lump in my throat and looked her in the eye. "From you."

Soon, I saw Sue, Jenny, and Haz in the background. And as they approached, Sue's kids running too, I didn't feel alone. Not at all.

Because these were my people now.

These were my *family* now.

"I was running away because I couldn't face up to the idea that all we're seeking out is shelter. Survival. I couldn't... I couldn't accept that there's no permanent solution. Not anymore."

"There might still be," Remy said.

"No," I said. "The longer we believe that, the more danger we put ourselves in."

"Just so you know," Haz said as he panted his way towards me. "You nearly killed me then. I haven't run like that since... well. Since ever."

I smiled. And I saw Sue smiling too, and then Remy, and Jenny, and Hannah, and the kids were laughing.

"The longer we run from the truth, the more danger we put ourselves in. We need to step up now. All of us. We need to be willing."

"Willing for what?" Sue asked.

I felt my heart racing and that urge I'd had all my life to step back into the background rising again.

But this time, I didn't let it take hold.

"Willing to fight," I said. "Willing to survive. Because from this point on, that's all there is left."

CHAPTER FORTY-ONE

Garry wasn't sure how long he'd been walking, only that he was certain he'd have to find some kind of safe place soon or he might not last much longer.

The walk had been intense. The sun was descending. He preferred the darkness. He wasn't sure why, exactly, just that it probably went back to when he was a kid. He used to hide under the stairs when his dad got home. He'd turn the lights on, shuffle his way as far under as possible, past the stacks of canned food and right to the back, where he was sure no one could get to him. Where he was too small to be reached.

Sometimes, his dad would know where he was. He'd try to get in there by pushing the cans against him, so he was pressed right up to the bottom of the stairs. His dad would laugh at him, telling him he was going to suffocate in there, but Garry never minded at all. He didn't have that same claustrophobia that apparently so many people struggled with. He felt solace in the darkness. Respite.

Some days, he'd spend all day under there. He'd eat the tinned peaches, open a little carnation cream and treat himself to it, even though his dad was stomping around the house, the threat of his presence constantly looming large.

But the saddest thing? The *darkest* thing?

Garry would always have to come out from under the stairs eventually.

And when he did...

"Garry?"

He shuddered, his attention returning when he heard the voice. When he turned around, he saw Mitch beside him. Mitch was looking thin. Sure, they had some food, but all their walking was taking it out of them.

And Garry knew that the longer they walked and the longer they stretched on without electricity or power, the longer they'd be free. But also, the longer that time stretched on, the more danger he and the people around him were in.

Mitch pointed down at his feet. "My feet, mate. I... I don't know how much further I can go."

"You're giving up?" Garry said.

Mitch shook his head. "Not giving up. I just... I dunno how much further I can go. We should rest up. Go again tomorrow."

"And when we go again tomorrow? What then? You think your wounds will be healed? You think everything will be back to normal."

"That's not what I said."

"You need to wake up, all four of you. You need to face it. When we're out here, it's going to be difficult. It's going to be impossible, even. But if we want to survive—if we want to flourish—we are going to have to do a lot of difficult things."

"Easy for you to say," Mitch muttered.

Garry turned and looked at him, frowning. "What did you say?"

Mitch lowered his head a little like he was trying to escape the spotlight. "Nothing."

"No," Garry said, stepping closer to him. "I want to hear what you just said. I want to know what you meant."

He stood right opposite him, now. He could smell the sourness of his breath, taste his sweat in the air. He could hear him breathing shakily. He knew he was weak. He didn't like weakness. It was a detestable property.

"Look at me," Garry said. "Look me in the eye and repeat what you just said."

After a few seconds, Mitch did look up and looked Garry right in the eye.

"I said it must be easy for you to say. Seeing as you've already killed people and done shitty things."

Garry smiled, then. He could feel the old prison order returning. He, the one who others bowed down to; the one others feared. He preferred things that way. He preferred being respected because he was someone who stood up and took control, and he liked it that way.

"You're right," Garry said. He put a hand on Mitch's shoulder and felt him flinch. "It does come easy to me. And really, when you look at it, it should come easily to you, too. I mean, you've had all the practice in the world, being locked up inside. You've seen people's inhumanity towards one another. And yet still you choose to squirm."

There was silence between them. But Garry could feel Mitch's heart picking up in pace.

"So are you strong enough?" Garry asked.

Mitch nodded, with uncertainty.

"Hey," Garry said, slapping Mitch's face. "I asked you a question. Are you strong enough?"

"Yes."

"What?"

"Yes!"

"Good," Garry said.

He took his hand off Mitch's shoulder.

Mitch had no idea that Garry's other hand had been on his knife, just in case.

He looked at the rest of his people, all four of them. They looked worn down. They looked like they'd been through hell.

But they had to be ready for what was next.

"Any others of you having problems knowing whether you're strong enough?"

They all looked at him with uncertainty.

And with fear.

"Is that a yes?"

"Yes," a couple of them said.

Garry exhaled, and he smiled.

"Good," he said. "Then we make our way to this safe zone. And when we get there, we blend in, and then in time, we take the place for ourselves."

He looked around at the setting sun, and he prepared to continue his walk onwards.

He had no idea he was on a collision course with another group.

Another group he'd clashed with before.

Another group he was looking forward to settling the score with very, very much...

CHAPTER FORTY-TWO

The next day, for the first time, everything felt good.

The mid-morning sun was shining brightly. Up ahead, I could see a nearby suburban village. Part of me wanted to go down there and explore it, because ultimately, not everywhere had gone to hell. That just couldn't be the case. It was something I wasn't willing to believe or to accept.

But whatever the case, we had made our decision.

And this time, it was a whole-hearted decision.

We weren't looking for some kind of shortcut anymore. We weren't seeking anyone who could magically make things better for us. We knew there was little chance of finding another safe zone, and if we did find another safe zone, there was a good chance it wouldn't offer much in the way of respite or security, just like the other ones we'd found.

We were taking responsibility for ourselves.

I was taking responsibility for myself.

"So what's the plan?" Hannah asked.

I looked at her, and I smiled as Lionel trotted alongside us. I saw Hannah was smiling, too. Her dark hair was swaying in the gentle breeze. She looked good. It was the first real time I'd actually acknowledged someone else looked good since the death of Harriet. I felt like I was betraying Harriet, just by having those feelings.

But I'd remembered what we'd said when we'd both had a conversation a long time ago about the big "what if?" something happened to either of us. Of course, the conversation had been light-hearted, not totally serious, but there had been a twinge of seriousness to every conversation like that.

"Well, you'll just have to become a nun, won't you?" I'd said.

She'd punched me, grinning at me with that gap-toothed smile. "You selfish git."

"So you'd really be so happy me just finding someone else myself?"

"Of course."

I'd frowned. "Really?"

"Well, don't get too many ideas just yet, mate. But obviously. If she made you happy, then that's what I'd want for you."

I'd leaned in, kissed her, tasted her lipstick. And as we'd lay there together, I'd really felt like the pair of us was forever. "I don't want anyone else," I'd said. "I never want anyone else."

Hannah clicked her fingers. "Hey. Snap out of it. What's up with you?"

I looked around at my surroundings. I must've zoned out. "Sorry. I just..."

"I asked you what the plan was now we've opted for the lonely wanderer route?"

"Well," I said, eager to get those thoughts of guilt and betrayal from my mind. "I was thinking about what I've seen on TV shows."

"Factual stuff? Like Bear Grylls?"

"Not exactly. You know, the prisons could be a good place to head to."

Hannah scoffed. "Prisons?"

"Think about it. What's the first thing prisoners do when the power goes down?"

"Smash skulls?"

"After smashing skulls."

"Well, escape."

"Exactly. So we've got a load of these well-defended buildings all across the country, all empty and waiting for people to inhabit them."

"Yeah. You've definitely been watching too much television."

"It's just a thought," I said. "Besides. Haz says it could be a good plan."

"Haz has watched too much television *and* played too many video games."

"But he knows his stuff," I said.

Hannah shrugged. "I guess I can't deny that."

"Where is Haz, anyway?"

I walked back to the rest of the group, past Remy, past Jenny—who we still didn't know a thing about—and past Sue and her kids. Haz was lingering behind.

"What're you up to?"

"Making a compass," Haz said.

He put a needle on a magnet. Then, he put a strip of foil on top of a cup of water—which I argued was wasteful for a few seconds until he said we could drink it anyway. He lifted the needle off the magnet and then placed it on top of the foil. The needle and foil spun around and pointed to our left.

"Pretty cool, right?" Haz asked.

I nodded, pleased to see Haz confident, and in his element. "Pretty cool. I just..."

Haz's face dropped. "What? What this time?"

I wanted to say "how do we know that's true north?" Instead, I decided to let Haz just have his moment. "No. It's great. Good job."

At that moment, it felt like Haz and I were closer than we'd been since meeting. It felt like the pieces of this group were clicking into place—even if Jenny was still a bit of a mystery. It felt like there was solidarity between us all; like, despite sacrificing some of ourselves by accepting our fates—that we probably weren't going to be saved—we were freer than we'd ever been.

I turned around to Hannah and went to rejoin the front of the group, keen to show her what I'd learned.

I saw someone else was there, standing right opposite her.

Another group. Five of them.

"Well well," a voice said, and I realised right then I knew this voice after all. "Fancy seeing you again, 'Scott'. I'm Garry. Pleasure to formally meet after our two little run-ins."

There was no denying it.

It was the prisoner who'd killed Jason.

And he and his people were all holding weapons.

CHAPTER FORTY-THREE

I stood opposite Garry and looked into his eyes, and he looked back into mine.

The clouds were forming over the sun, foreshadowing impending doom. Or perhaps it was just the coincidental turn of the weather. Perhaps there was nothing more to it.

But somehow, it felt timely.

Hannah, Haz, and Remy stood by my side. Sue stood further back with Jenny—who was still not up to strength just yet—and the kids. There was a silence about the place, both our group and Garry's group. There were four people with him, one of whom I recognised from the stand-off with Jason, and the incident in Derek's house. I didn't know what had happened to Garry in his time on the road, what *might* have happened to him. I didn't want to think about it, not really. Not with the look in his eyes right now.

And Sue still didn't know this was the man who killed her husband; who left her children fatherless.

"So," Garry said, his intense stare shifting into something resembling a smile. "Where you folks heading to?"

He asked it as if it was no issue at all; like we were old friends just catching up with one another after a long time of absence.

"We're heading our way," I said, standing my ground, holding my hands in fists. "You should head yours."

Garry smiled like he was carefully considering my words, weighing them up, searching them for hidden meaning. "Yeah. Yeah, we are. But I think it's pretty beautiful that after all this time, all this distance, it's back to you and me again. Right?"

I felt my heart racing. The old me screamed in my ear to step aside, to give up, to stop staring Garry in his eyes.

But the old me's voice wasn't as loud anymore. Not after the things I'd done. Not after the way I'd watched Derek fall, then the way I'd shot Garry's friend.

Not after the incident at Margery and Bill's house.

"You see, the last time we saw you, you made it even, if you remember rightly. One each."

"What's he talking about?" Sue said. "What does he mean 'one each'?"

"Oh, hello," Garry said, leaning around me and acknowledging the rest of the group for the first time. "I don't remember seeing you last time. You were there, though, right? When your friend here shot one of my people?"

"You said you made it even," Sue said, determination in her voice. "What do you mean by that?"

"Sue. Leave it," I said.

Then I saw Garry looking between me and Sue, the cogs in his mind turning once again as he tried to add things up, as he tried to work things out.

I hoped he wouldn't. I prayed he wouldn't make the link.

But then I saw the shift in his eyes, and I knew he was onto it.

"Oh," he said, a smirk stretching across his face. "Oh, shit!"

"Scott, what's he talking about?" Sue asked.

"Don't," I said to Garry. "Please."

Garry chuckled a little. Then he went to walk around me,

towards Sue, towards her kids.

I don't know what possessed me to do so, but I stepped in his way and pressed my gun against him.

He stopped, just inches from my face. I could feel his breathing getting more rapid. And his face didn't have that comical look anymore. He looked genuinely threatened by the way I was standing up to him.

"Don't," I said. "Just go your way, and we go ours. We're even. Like you said."

Garry tilted his head to one side and smiled. He lifted a hand, put it on my gun. "Oh, Scott. You see, I'd love for that to happen. I really would. But I'm not used to getting *even*..."

Then, he lifted a knife and pressed it to my neck. His face shifted completely.

"So why don't you tell her? Why don't you turn around and tell her and her children what happened back at the house?"

I swallowed a lump in my throat. I wanted to push back, to fight.

But I couldn't.

I just couldn't.

I turned around. I looked Hannah in the eyes, first. I couldn't get a read on her.

So I looked past her and at Sue. At her two kids.

I saw them looking back at me, and I knew this was the moment their innocence was going to disappear, what with what I knew, with what I'd done.

"Sue," I said. "I'm sorry."

"Scott?" She said. "What is it? What's wrong?"

"I—"

"Scott here ducked when I swung at your dear husband," Garry interrupted, yanking the gun rapidly from my hand. "And guess who just so happened to be standing behind his cowardly back?"

More lack of understanding.

More confusion in Sue's eyes.

Then she dropped to her knees, and it clicked.

"No," she said.

And I expected to see that grief take over her once again.

But it didn't.

Instead, she started running towards Garry angrily, the second of our remaining guns raised.

"No!" she shouted.

I tried to step in her way, to stop her. "Sue!"

But it was too late.

One second, she was flying at Garry.

The next, Garry was turning his knife to her.

I didn't watch as she landed on it. I couldn't hear anything but the screams of her children anyway.

But when I turned around, when I came to my senses, Sue was on the ground.

Garry wiped his blade on his coat, then picked up the gun that had fallen from Sue's hand. He looked over at me, and he smiled.

"Now, we're even," he said.

Remy was on his knees. Hannah looked mortified. Haz was crying.

I was on the verge of giving up.

But as I watched Sue's children run over to her, as I saw the pain and the lack of understanding on their horrified faces, I felt something take over me.

That word, again.

"No," I said.

Garry turned around. As did the rest of his people. "What?" he said.

I stood up. Took in a deep breath. I reached into my pocket and pulled out a penknife.

"I said no. We're not even."

The next thing I knew, I was swinging the penknife at Garry's neck.

CHAPTER FORTY-FOUR

I swung the blade at Garry's neck and waited for the blood to spurt out of it, with no feelings of shame, no feelings of guilt, no feelings of fear, not anymore.

But nothing came out of his neck.

Nothing, because he raised a hand and batted the penknife away like it was nothing.

Then he punched me in the gut.

I fell to my knees, winded and crippled. I gasped for air as my knees squelched in the dirt. I didn't want to give up fighting. I didn't want to give in to this bully.

When I looked up at him, I saw he had that wry smile on his face like he knew he was in the ascendancy after all.

"See, that's your problem," Garry said, looming large over me, gun in hand. "You pretend you're strong. You try to convince yourself you're some kind of warrior; some kind of fighter. But you are not."

He threw my knife aside, and before I had the time to process what was happening, he sent a piledriver right across my face.

I slammed back into the dirt. I could taste blood building in the back of my mouth. Broken teeth chipped against my tongue. If I weren't careful, I'd choke on it.

I tried to get back up. I could see the rest of my people were on their knees now, too. Jenny. Sue's children. Haz. Hannah.

I looked over at Hannah through my bruised, squinting eyes, and I saw her looking back at me with fear. And that look in her eyes terrified me because it looked to me like a loss of hope. A surrender to other people; people who were stronger than us. People who were willing to do the things that we weren't willing to do.

I wasn't able to look at Hannah much longer because I felt a boot crack against my face, and I went flying back into the squelchy, wet mud.

My ears rang. Pain crippled my face. All I could taste was blood, and all I could see was the blurry silhouette of Garry, who was above me.

He leaned in towards me, then wrapped his hands around my neck.

"The thing about you is, you might think you can step up and be a leader. You might *think* you have it in you to do all the nasty, awful things this world requires. But believe me, you do not. And I'm gonna kill you with my bare hands. Believe me, I am. But only after I've made you watch me and my people take your friends out, one by one. Let's see how much faith they have in their leader when you're made to watch them die, hmm?"

Your friends.

He tightened his hands around my neck, and I felt my consciousness waning right away. I struggled to breathe, battled to inhale, to exhale.

But his hands just kept getting tighter.

He smirked at me, and I saw the beast behind his eyes. Really, that's all this man was. He'd been a beast before the power went out, and he was a beast now the power had gone out. Only the world was a playground for beasts like him, now. They were the ones at the top of the food chain. They were the ones to fear.

He pulled his hands away, and I gasped for dear life.

He didn't give me long.

He punched me again, this time hard enough to make me black out for a few seconds. I knew I'd blacked out because the next thing I knew, he was a few metres away from me, walking over to my friends, gun in hand.

"So who shall we go for first?" Garry said. He looked along the line, all of them kneeling. "How about this one?"

He pointed at Haz.

I felt my chest tense up.

Then he lowered the gun, moved further along the line.

"Or maybe this one. Maybe this little girl here."

"Please," Hannah said.

He turned to Hannah then. He walked over to her, looked right down at her.

"What did you just say?"

"I said please," she said. "Don't hurt the children. Anyone but them. Please."

Garry paused for a few seconds. "That's interesting," he said. "You know, last time we met, I didn't quite finish with you. I think we should catch up. Continue where we left off. How's that sound, hmm?"

He nodded at his people.

All of them kicked down my friends.

All of them but Hannah.

Garry grabbed her by the hair. He dragged her towards me, then he threw her to her knees, right in front of me.

"You'll look into her eyes," Garry said. "When this happens, you'll look right into her eyes."

I felt helpless as tears streamed down Hannah's face.

I felt weak like I couldn't do a thing.

"I'm sorry," I said.

But right away when I said that word, "sorry," I knew it wasn't enough.

Garry crouched down towards Hannah.

"You'll watch her—"

He didn't say another word. And it didn't click properly at first, not even though I'd been the one to stop him speaking.

I'd punched him in the face as hard as I could.

He held his cheek. Then he looked back at me, slightly alarmed.

"What did you just—"

I punched him again.

Even though I was weak, worn down, broken and bruised, I kept on punching back, kept on fighting. I could see my people struggling with the rest of Garry's people, who clearly didn't know how to control the situation.

When I'd punched and kicked at Garry again, I scrambled for the knife of mine he'd thrown down, which was just metres from me.

I wrapped my hand around it.

Garry stamped on my hand.

He looked down at me, and he smiled, gun pointing down at me. But this time, his smile had nothing in it but pure malice. Like he was going to enjoy what he was about to do.

But I didn't feel fear. Not anymore.

I just felt...

"Garry. One of them's..."

I didn't hear the rest of what one of Garry's people said.

I just saw a window of opportunity—a window where I had no choice but to act—and I exploited it.

I punched Garry between the legs with my free hand. Hard.

The punch made him slip off my hand.

I scrambled for the blade.

Wrapped my hands around it.

Then before Garry could punch at me again, I stabbed it through his shoulder.

The cry of pain was instant. I felt a hot splatter of blood cover me as Garry dropped the gun instinctively and tried to yank the blade from his body.

But I was pushing. Hard, now.

I felt no shame.

I felt no fear.

Only justice.

I was on my feet, now. I was weak, but I was standing. Over the top of Garry, I could see my people still on their knees. But the other prisoners weren't looking at them. They weren't doing anything.

They were just looking over at me and Garry with shock.

I looked into Garry's eyes. And from the way he was looking at me, as I pulled out the knife, I knew I had that same look I'd seen in his eyes.

That animalistic look.

"You're wrong," I said.

Then I slammed the blade into the middle of his chest.

"I'll do whatever it takes to keep my people safe."

He coughed up blood. He spluttered. He took a weak swing at me, then just fell to his knees.

When he'd fallen, he looked up at me, blood rolling down his chin.

"You'll live with this," he muttered. "You'll... you'll live with this forever."

"I don't doubt it," I said. "But you won't."

Then I took a final swing with the knife, and I ended Garry's life, right there.

Silence followed. The wind brushed through the grounds. Nobody said a word.

Garry's people looked on, stunned.

"Well?" I said. "Do you want the same thing to happen to you?"

They looked at one another like they were plotting a move in retaliation.

Then, at the same time, all of them turned around, and all of them ran.

I hobbled over to Hannah. I held out a hand, helped her back to her feet.

"Scott, you don't look good."

I ignored her, and I made my way over to Sue's side.

I dropped beside her and looked down into her open eyes.

Then I put a hand on her stomach, which was still warm.

"I'm sorry," I said.

I went to close her eyes.

"I'm—"

I felt myself dizzying. I felt myself losing consciousness.

But in my last moments, I swore I saw Sue open her eyes, and heard her splutter...

CHAPTER FORTY-FIVE

"Do you think we'll ever live in a normal world again?"

When I heard Holly's words, all I could do was look at her and smile, like her question was about something fantastical, like Santa Claus or tooth fairies. And the only way I could act was by delivering the same kind of answer as I did about those two topics, too. "Maybe. If you behave well for your mum."

Holly tilted her head like she was considering what I was saying.

I looked ahead of me, out of the window of the house where we were staying. We'd been walking for a week since the incident with Garry, and eventually, we'd found a home in the suburbs that was empty and had a few supplies left.

Of course, it wouldn't be a permanent setup. Soon, we would have to move on because nowhere and nothing was permanent now.

Our lives were just jumping from one safe place to the next. Or at least, one place with the *illusion* of safety to the next.

And there was no other way about it.

I stood up when I saw Sue walking into the room. She was

holding her son's hand. It was a miracle she'd survived at all after Garry stabbed her and she'd fallen unconscious. I was so convinced she was dead that I'd gone to close her eyes, only for her to cough up blood and splutter back to life.

Her survival was a miracle, especially with the lack of sanitation. But Sue was wrong when she said she wasn't a survivor. She was. And this was proof.

We'd all pulled together. We'd all fought to keep her alive.

And here she was, still here for her children, still here for the group.

"All okay downstairs?" I asked.

Sue nodded and smiled. "All good."

I nodded back at her, then walked past her, heading towards the landing area and down the stairs.

"Scott?"

I turned back.

Sue looked at me closely, intently. "I never thanked you."

I frowned. "For what?"

"For killing the man who killed their father. Thank you."

Sue's words were said with such gratitude, so much so that they made the hairs on my arms stand on end. After all, she was talking about someone's death. A death that I had been responsible for and not the first.

But similarly, I sensed a strength building in Sue, as she stood beside her two children, united, together, *alive*.

"I'd do it again in a heartbeat," I said.

The scary thing?

I said those words with complete honesty.

I walked down the landing area, down towards the lounge. On my way, I saw Remy in his room. He looked at me, nodded his head, and I nodded right back at him.

"How's the face?" he asked.

"Still sore," I said. "Still a tooth or two short. But I'll live."

He nodded again, with absolute seriousness. "That's a good thing. Really."

As I made my way downstairs, towards the kitchen, I could smell the food coming from the stove already. It was a portable stove, which meant we were technically only cooking things the way we cooked them outside. But there was something about a *home* that made the whole experience completely different. Something about being inside that really made me and all of us feel... well. A degree of normality that was otherwise robbed from us by this world.

When I got to the kitchen, I saw Jenny and Haz sitting at the table, Haz practically salivating—over the food or Jenny, I couldn't be certain.

Standing over the stove, Hannah.

She looked around at me and smiled right away. "Fancy seeing you here."

"Where else would I be?"

"When there's food around? Yep. I supposed you've got me."

Lionel came running at me. I ruffled his fur, tickled his back, which he always loved. Then I took a seat near Haz and Jenny. "How're we for water?"

Haz tilted his head to one side. "We've been better. But we can head for a stream just down the road later. Check this out I've made."

Has had made a filter using a plastic bottle, a coffee filter, some charcoal, sand, and gravel. The idea was to filter the water through several natural layers before boiling to totally clean it. I was still amazed at Haz's level of knowledge. It was really quite something.

"You know, I'll never know how you do it."

"Do what?"

"Retain all this useless information."

He chuckled. Jenny laughed, too.

"Not so useless now, though, is it?" he asked.

I smiled back. "I guess not."

I sat there a little longer, and I watched Hannah make the food. She turned around a couple of times, smiled at me. And every time she did that, I felt like I really could move on. Like I didn't have to stay stuck in the past. Like I could honour Harriet's wishes after all and fall for someone new.

But falling for someone had its dangers, too. Namely the fact that we'd opted for survival, constantly on the move, ahead of searching for some kind of hypothetical extraction point that probably didn't even exist. That had put us at an advantage.

It was a tough pill to swallow. But swallow it, we had to.

We all sat at the table an hour or so later and tucked into the rabbit stew, the rabbits of which we'd caught ourselves. And as the sun set, I didn't feel fear anymore. I didn't feel helpless. I felt more together with other people than I'd ever done before.

"I like it here," Hannah said when we were tucking into the last of our meal.

"Yeah," I said. "Me too."

"Do you think maybe... maybe we'll be able to stay here?"

I sighed and half-smiled. I had to be real. "No. I don't. Because I think the second we believe that's possible, we put ourselves at a disadvantage."

She looked back at me as if the moment's fantasy had gone, evaporated, in an instant. "Cheers, killjoy."

I raised a glass of wine and chinked hers. "My pleasure."

We joked about it, but we knew it was true. Soon, we would move on from this place. We would hunt. We would find water. We would scavenge, and we would do all kinds of uncomfortable things, all because we wanted one thing more than anything—to survive.

But we would never forget our humanity.

As difficult as it was to cling onto your morals when you had killed people... when the images wouldn't stop flashing in your mind... I kept on praying that I'd be able to hold on to that humanity and morality forever.

"I just thought of something," Hannah said.

"And what's that?" I asked, growing more intoxicated by the wine, more drawn towards her, more tempted by that voice in my head to make my move and have no regrets.

She smiled back at me. "When my Kindle lost charge. I just realised had a paperback book packed all along."

She laughed, and I laughed too. And then I heard Haz and Jenny start to laugh, and before I knew it everyone was in this kitchen, all of us smiling, all of us laughing, all of us together.

Because that's what we were now. Together.

And that's *who* we were now.

We were the survivors.

And we were going to make this world work in our favour. No matter what it took.

WANT MORE FROM RYAN CASEY?

The World After: Book 2 is now available to buy.

If you want to be notified when Ryan Casey's next novel in The World After series is released (and receive a free book from his Dead Days post apocalyptic series), please sign up for the mailing list by going to: http://ryancaseybooks.com/fanclub Your email address will never be shared and you can unsubscribe at any time.

Word-of-mouth and reviews are crucial to any author's success. If you enjoyed this book, please leave a review. Even just a couple of lines sharing your thoughts on the story would be a fantastic help for other readers.

20632626R00132

Printed in Poland
by Amazon Fulfillment
Poland Sp. z o.o., Wrocław